SUCH LOVELY SKIN

SUCH LOVELY SKIN

TATIANA SCHLOTE-BONNE

First published in 2024 by
Page Street Publishing Co.
27 Congress Street, Suite 1511
Salem, MA 01970

www.pagestreetpublishing.com

Distributed by Macmillan, sales in Canada by The Canadian Manda Group.

28 27 26 25 24 1 2 3 4 5

ISBN-13: 979-8-89003-076-4

Library of Congress Control Number: 2023949949

Cover and book design by Emma Hardy for Page Street Publishing Co.
Cover image © Tess Hamilton

Printed and bound in the United States

Page Street Publishing protects our planet by donating to nonprofits like The Trustees, which focuses on local land conservation.

CONTENT WARNING:

child death and mentions of suicide

I lie in bed, editing my Twitch bio on my phone:

half-Japanese, half-elf | she/her | part-time witch | full-time streamer | total screwup somebody kill me plz

I delete that last part even though it's how I feel all day every day. My bio now ends with "full-time streamer," which feels like a lie since I don't stream anymore, but I remind myself that's still who I am—well, was—before I ruined everyone's lives three months ago.

My phone vibrates.

Brianna: hey viv!! holding up ok??😊

I reply: i'm ok :)) you???

Brianna: good!!!

The three dots tell me she's still typing. I hope she's just sending a SpongeBob meme or something funny, nothing that engages with the fact that school starts on Monday.

Brianna: sooo just wanted to throw it out there—Mason's throwing a party tonight to celebrate the last weekend before senior year. you're totally welcome to come!!!! no pressure, but I MISS YOU GIRL

My stomach sinks. The old me would've loved to go. But a party at Mason's means everyone will be there. And since it's the Saturday before school, it'll be a rager.

I start to type: idk I think I'm getting the flu because it's easier to lie than admit that I just don't want to go, then I mash the delete button. *Why not go?*

Because it would mean putting on pants and brushing my hair, and those two things combined would be harder than beating a *Dark Souls* boss with my real-life bare hands. Plus, everyone will pity me, and I don't deserve anyone's sympathy. That's the worst part of it all: No one—not my parents, not even Bri—knows I'm the one to blame for what happened in June. I was never super popular, but before all this happened, I at least had my thing: I was the Horror Gamer Girl. Now I'm just the girl who suffered a horrible loss. If I go to Mason's, I'll be the embodiment of a party pooper. #tragedy.

I reply: idk. i'll think about it

Instantly, I feel bad for letting Bri down. She's been so

supportive during this time—coming to feed me, sending me funny memes, checking in constantly—and I have no idea what's going on in her life anymore. The Friday before that terrible day in June, we played *Magic: The Gathering Arena*, and she gave me all the spicy details about how she and Eric finally went to bonetown. For the past three months, I've been a miserable slug she checks up on, and I'm sure it's getting annoying. *I'm* even annoyed with me. I send a few smiley emojis just to show that maybe there is some hope.

Brianna: ok!!!

Brianna: have you thought about streaming at all?

Brianna: or we could just hang out and play magic again!!

Brianna: but maybe streaming something would be good for you?? you know, jump back on that virtual horse

I send a "love" reaction to all of her texts. Of course I've thought about my return to streaming. It's the only thing on my mind other than my guilt. But I don't know if I have it in me to put on the performance, and even if I could prop myself in front of the camera and laugh and act like everything's fine—what would I play? It would need to be a new game. Something fresh. Something that screams *Hello, I'm Back and Worth Your Time*. Instead of a party, maybe that's what I need the weekend before school: a new horror game. If I can bring my channel back to life, maybe I can start getting out of bed before noon and live with myself.

I sit up and scroll through my email. I used to get messages all the time from viewers asking me to play the obscure indie they'd programmed in their basement. The creator always appreciates the free marketing, and the niche indie games make my channel different from the million *League of Legends* streamers. Maybe there's a gem lingering in all my unread emails, something scary and perfect for my return to Twitch.

There's a link to a hentai game. Some 2D fruit-collecting game. Another sex game. A game that's basically the poor man's *Baldur's Gate 3*. A subject line that says PLAY THIS GAME NOW!!! IT WILL CHANGE YOUR LIFE!!! It's been sent dozens—no, fifty-four—times from the same spam email: c00lg4m3rs123@yahoo.com. My thumb hovers over the message. There's something appealing about the shameless desperation of the subject line. I figure it's fifty-fifty chance that it's actually an intriguing game instead of a virus. Before I can overthink it, I open the email. Over a black background, it reads:

Introducing LOCKED IN: An Escape Room Horror Game! Play only if you dare to face your darkest fears!!!

The game's cover art shows a cartoon girl crouched in a hallway corner, her eyelids and mouth sewn shut. Totally my vibe. I click the link to the website, chewing my thumbnail as the page loads. A few comments on the site call the game "edgy and scary" and "claustrophobic," possibly left by the programmer themself. True or not, edgy and claustrophobic are my jam. And even if the game sucks, I can just rip on it with my fans, like I'm the gamer version of Tom Servo in an *MST3K* episode.

I glance at the lighting, webcam, and mic setup at my desk, all of which have grown dusty. I've been gaming during my grieving period, but offline and on my laptop in bed. *The Sims. Skyrim. New Vegas.* The comfort foods of gaming. I walk to my desk and wiggle the mouse. Once the screen comes to life, I load the *LOCKED IN* website. The Download for Free button stares back at me. The home page's piano number plays through my speakers, a soft melodic tune. A little girl hums in the background.

Could this be it? My return to the screen? My return to what makes me *me*?

Excitement tingles down my limbs to my fingers, a feeling I haven't experienced in months. I slide into the hot pink ergonomic gaming chair I bought with my own Twitch paycheck after I broke 30,000 followers and 100 paid subscribers. I stretch my neck side to side, then click the download button. I'll do a practice run now, then maybe—if I can really go through with it—I'll start streaming once I have all the functions figured out.

The opening menu loads. The game options are written in the same cheesy red font as the email, and the soft piano number with the humming girl plays once more. It's so cliché, but hey, creepy little girls *are* scary. I click New Game. My avatar spawns in a narrow hallway, the windows boarded up, the yellow floral wallpaper peeling off the walls. The graphics are surprisingly high-quality and realistic. Something jagged is protruding out of the wallpaper. I zoom in closer. Fingernails—broken and bloody. Love it.

The hallway continues into darkness, too dark for me to see what's ahead. I hit Tab to increase the gamma, but a flashlight flickers to life in my avatar's hand, illuminating the long stretch of hallway that ends in a stairwell. I turn to my left. Another long stretch of hallway. *Creeaak.* I whip the camera toward the noise. A figure dressed in dark robes steps out of a room and ascends the stairs so quickly I don't get a good look at them. I move in that direction, but the journal log opens, stopping me in place.

I read the message aloud, practicing my delivery for an imaginary Twitch audience.

You are a reporter investigating rumors of malevolent spirits in an abandoned apartment complex. The way you entered has been sealed shut. Your presence has awoken something in the building that does not want you to leave alive.

Hide. Run. Escape.

"You hear that, guys?" I say to my pretend viewers. "Trapped in a haunted building. Nothing we haven't handled before." I used to feel awkward talking to myself like this, but now I can't game at all without imagining a streamer script, which is good. It's kept me from getting too rusty.

A message appears in the right corner: **Find Batteries.**

The flashlight flickers, its beam of light narrowing. I enter the nearest room. A torn rug covers the wooden floor. A cracked TV hangs from the wall. Nothing's glowing or blinking to tell me it's an important object, and that's how I like my games: no hand-holding. I open the kitchen drawers.

You find nothing.

I search the pile of junk on the table.

You find nothing.

The flashlight flickers more aggressively, going out for three seconds before coming back to life with a shake. I head for the bedroom and open the dresser.

You find nothing.

Oh, come on. But I have to admit, I respect a game that doesn't give everything to me too easily. I search the nightstand.

Batteries added to inventory.

Finally. I drag the batteries over to the flashlight and the beam shines brighter. I turn around and jolt—a girl in a white nightie crouches in the upper right corner of the room in full crab pose: back arched, crawling upside down. She scutters up the wall and across the ceiling, disappearing into the closet, giggling. Hardly original, but effective. I shake the spookies off and head back out to the hallway.

The nice thing about streaming is that it's not like I'm playing alone. These kinds of games are always *waaay* scarier offline. But I'm into it. Being on edge like this makes me feel more alive than I have in months. Besides, when I get really creeped out by a game, I take Bakugo out of his tank to keep me company.

I slide my gaming chair over to the dresser, where Bakugo lounges on the heated rock in his glass tank. He's a ghost boa, his scales a light milky gray. Mom pitched a fit when I told her I was getting him, but I bought him with my own money, and since he stays in my room all the time, she never even has to acknowledge his existence.

I place Bakugo on my shoulder, and he slithers beneath my hair into a loop around my neck, his scales cool and comforting. Now I'm ready to dig deep into this game. There are three other doors on this floor. Two are cobwebbed and the other is riddled with claw marks, like a bear tried to slash its way through. Obviously, that's the winner. I enter the room. The door clicks shut on its own behind me. I turn around to open it again, but the knob only rattles. Locked. Cool, something important is definitely here. A puzzle I have to solve.

I pan my camera across the room. A grandfather clock ticks in the corner. The flashlight illuminates an old, sagging couch marred with blotchy rust-colored stains. A painting of an older woman hangs on the wall, her hands folded, a feathery hat on her head. Of course her eyes follow me as I turn to the right.

The metronomic beats of the grandfather clock start going faster, filling my speakers with a rapid *tick, tick, tick*. I try clicking on the clock, but nothing happens. I step back and look around the room again. Bakugo's coil tightens around my neck. Someone is sitting on the couch now. They're dressed in black robes. Beady orange eyes stare back at me from beneath the dark cloak. Hello, creepy.

I don't have any weapons, so combat wouldn't be ideal. I imagine I'm streaming and ask my viewers what I should do next. The chat would suggest I "go into sneak mode," "turn the flashlight off," "just fight the NPC you noob!!!"

Direct confrontation it is. I do a quick save. Worst-case scenario: I die and reload. I don't even pretend to be one of those pretentious anti-save scummers. I click on the NPC. It stands slowly, using the couch to lift itself up like its joints ache. Surprisingly realistic animation for a budget indie game. The NPC takes a couple jarring, quick steps toward me. A text box appears: **To escape the room, you must tell me a secret.**

A secret? I wonder how that works—like, if the program scans what I type for certain key phrases, or maybe it doesn't matter at all. I can just mash the keyboard.

"Oooh guys, you hear that?" I say to my imagined streamer audience. "It wants a seeecret."

A dark secret.

"Oooh, hear that, guys?" I follow up with my imagined audience. "A daaaark secret." But I have to admit, the words "dark secret" spike my pulse. Of course, that day in June is the first thing that comes to mind. But telling this NPC my darkest secret is insane—right? I try to walk to the other side of the room to see if there's another way out, but my character is frozen in place. I could log out, but I've never given up so easily on a game. I start to type out some nonsense about how I once saw my mom making out with the neighbor next door—a total lie but it seems dark-secrety enough. I hit Enter.

Darker.

I roll my eyes.

And true.

Okay, that's creepy. And nice props to the creator. They must've assumed everyone would make up some BS on their first input. I write the one-sentence summary of what happened in June, then reach for the backspace. I hesitate.

Why not hit Send?

I downloaded this game. It's completely offline. No one's ever going to see these words other than me. Typing out the truth would almost be like talking about it to someone. This NPC can be my therapy bot, and maybe I do need to talk about what happened, since the only form of therapy I had was with the grief counselor that my parents and I had a handful of sessions with before it got too expensive and who I lied to anyway.

Before I can overthink it, I read the words one more time, then I hit Enter.

I killed my baby sister.

Tell me more.

After word-vomiting out eight paragraphs detailing the steps leading up to Riley's death that day and all the unspeakable things I did, I hit Enter and scoot back from the desk, blowing my nose and wiping my eyes. I toss the tissue onto the overflowing trash can of Kleenex. The NPC still hasn't responded, which I find extremely anticlimactic for baring my soul and admitting I'm the worst person alive. I unloop Bakugo from my neck and gently place him back in his tank. Finally, the NPC replies.

You may pass.

Wow. So cool. But I guess that's what I get for confessing my darkest secret to a cheap program. The NPC gestures toward a new door that's formed in the wall, but I'm too drained to keep playing now. I close the game, collapse onto my bed, and sob into my pillow, but something is different.

For the first time since Riley died, I finally told the truth about what happened. Sure, it might've been typed out in a game, but I've put the horrible event into words instead of just replaying it over and over and over in my mind. I feel lighter, like a few pounds from the anvil of guilt crushing my chest have been shaved off.

I fall into a deep post-cry nap, and when I wake, I have a new text from Bri.

just got to Mason's! it would totally make my day if you showed up!!! ♥

I drink a glass of water. *You can do this, you can do this, you can do this.* I dribble a couple Visine drops into my eyes, then I reply to Bri: on my way!

Blue hair requires a dedicated care routine that's hard enough to upkeep even in the best circumstances—throw in the loss of will to live, and you get a matted greenish-gray-hag-witch look. I sit in my car outside Mason's house, plucking at my crispy swamp-creature locks in the rearview mirror. There's no salvaging this. I take a black beanie out of my purse, pull it over my head, and pray my thick dark eyeliner is enough to make me look decent.

I get out of my old Honda Civic and stand on the driveway, looking up at Mason's three-story lake house. Cool air blows off the water behind the house, the evening sunset glinting off the home's many windows. Mason's dad is the big real estate agent in town, so he owns, like, everything from the gas station to the apartments we lived in before Dad's HVAC business got off the ground. Must be nice.

I text Brianna: here!!!

She'd offered to pick me up when I said I was coming, but I wanted to drive myself in case I need to bail. I step forward, wiping my sweaty palms on my jeans, which feel too loose since I lost my appetite after Riley's death and my subsequent bedridden days. I walk across the lawn, my hips and back aching. These might be the most steps I've taken in weeks. Honestly, I'm lucky I don't have bed sores.

I cross the side of the house, and there are at least fifteen of my classmates hanging out on the dock, shouting and laughing. My pulse increases at the sight of other humans. I've only been isolated in my room for eleven weeks, but it feels like an eternity. Will I remember how to make small talk? Or how to act normal? Probably not, because I'm not normal anymore: I'm a baby killer—actually a *toddler* killer since Riley was almost three—and everyone else is still a nice, plain Midwestern teenager.

The boys whistle and cheer as a girl in a red bikini—it must be Lauren Miller with that platinum bleached hair—swings from a rope on a tree and splashes into the water. A couple more volleyball players leap from the rope into the lake, and I'm not sure if I'm jealous of their fun, judging this activity, or just indifferent to it all because nothing matters anymore.

No one's noticed me yet, which is nice, but I don't want to stand here all evening like a ghost haunting the party. . . . Okay, maybe I do. But I came here for Bri, and I don't want to flake. Where is she? I scan the dock but don't recognize her dark skin and signature high braided ponytail. She'd be pretty easy to spot if she were out there since there aren't many Black girls in our school. Ugh. I should've had her meet me at the car. I take a few steps forward.

Snap.

I turn to my left. Ash Torrance steps out from the trees, his eyes red-rimmed behind his black-framed glasses, a skunky waft of weed following him.

"Hey." He gives an awkward little wave and sideswipes his shoulder-length sandy-blond hair. "Didn't expect to see you coming to party at rich boy's house." His voice softens. "Sorry to hear about . . ."

I shrug. "It's cool. I've uh—" I look around, praying for Bri to swoop in and save me.

"VIV! Up here!" Bri yells from afar.

I glance up to my right and find Bri sticking her head out a second-story window. *Thank god.*

"Gotta go!" I say to Ash.

"See ya." He pulls a pack of cigarettes out of his baggy pants pocket.

I turn toward the house. What teen smokes cigarettes these days? Ash Torrance, of course, and I feel a little bad for judging him. He's probably the one person who would understand my loss the most since he's basically our town's tragedy. Four years ago, Ash's dad drove drunk and killed two nurses who were crossing the street after their shift. Ash's dad has been in prison ever since. At first, all of Merton, Iowa, oozed pity for Ash, but then he went all goth and decked himself out in satanic symbols and started smoking everything smokable. Once he didn't fit the nice Midwestern norm anymore, people's sympathy for him evaporated. I don't want everyone to pity me either—but I definitely don't want to be socially ostracized like Ash. I sprint away from him like he has Ebola and into the house.

I step through the kitchen and hesitate. Ten feet in front of me, past the marble island counter, are a dozen of my classmates drinking, chatting, laughing. *Can I do this? Can I really hang out with everyone and pretend that I'm fine?* The comfort of my room, Bakugo, my werewolf family in *The Sims*—they call to me, begging me to come back to their safety. I take a step backward. Then Hector Marquez notices me, his eyes widening. He whispers to Stephanie Williams beside him, and then everyone else looks to see who they're talking about. All eyes are on me, conversations slowing to a stop. I raise my right hand and give a small wave, trying to smile like I'm totally fine.

Everyone stares.

Our high school has about 700 students, mostly from white mid- to upper-middle class families, and it's been largely trauma-free since Ash's thing, so I get it. I was already one of three racially ambiguous people, and now I'm the only one with a dead sister too—so yeah, I'm a walking anomaly. Thankfully, the part where I killed her is my knowledge alone, or I'd be facing way worse than just some gawking.

Finally, Hector Marquez says, "'Sup, Viv?"

"How's it going? How's umm . . ." I grasp for the sport he's in or the name of his mother—something, anything to end the awful silence—but I'm coming up blank. ". . . your summer?"

"Pretty chill. Yours?" His face immediately fills with regret, and I internally flinch.

"Fine," I say. "Really, it's been fine." Great. Now does it sound like I don't care that my sister died?

More silence.

"VIV!" Bri rushes downstairs, her chunky pink platform sandals clomping with each step, her black braided ponytail swinging behind her. She shoots glances at everyone, her eyes telling them to *act normal*! And once they see her, conversations resume. She probably warned everyone about not making my return to society weird. Bless her.

Bri throws her arms around me. "You made it!"

I hug her back, squeezing like I haven't seen her in forever, even though she brought me Dairy Queen last Thursday night.

She's visited my house at least once a week if not more, but this is the first time we've seen each other out in the wild since June.

Eric walks down the stairs, catching up to Bri. "Hey, good to see you," he says to me, slinking a hand around Bri's waist. "Bri's missed her other half. And I'm glad you're doing better too. . . . You are, right?" His blue eyes fill with concern.

"Yeah, I'm good! It's nice to see you too." I give him a fist bump.

His stiff shoulders relax. "So you getting back into *Magic* again?" He runs a hand through his floppy auburn hair. "I'm getting tired of Bri kicking my ass all the time."

Bri playfully rolls her eyes.

"Yeah." I look to her. "Let's play . . . tomorrow?"

"Um, yes." Bri's face brightens so much, I regret that I've neglected our *Magic: The Gathering* nights for this long. We started playing it in the first place back in ninth grade so Bri could have something to say to Eric: the tall, blue-eyed himbo nerd and renowned *Magic* player in our school's gaming club. Then of course, Bri and I became the best players in the club. She beat Eric in the end of the semester tournament our freshman year, and they've been an item ever since.

Eric walks over to the fridge, grabbing a can of Truly.

"Want one?" Eric looks to me and Bri.

"Sure."

"Strawberry lemonade!" Bri says.

Eric tosses a can to each of us. I crack mine open, savoring the cold, fruity liquid, but the strawberry flavor only makes me remember how Riley loved strawberries and would sob-scream when Mom wouldn't let her eat the stems. But the stems are edible. I just learned that two weeks ago while watching a Netflix cooking show. Riley could've had those stems all along. I gulp down half the drink, the alcohol already making my limbs warm and heavy.

Bri takes my hand, pulling me to the den, where our classmates are singing karaoke and making TikToks of this hot mess. A girl whose name I can't remember but recognize from pre-calc sings a very shrill "Total Eclipse of the Heart." I plop down on the couch, sipping my drink.

After another song, Bri hops up. "Grabbing snacks and more drinks!"

"Don't leave me here long." I sink into the couch, making myself small.

Stephanie Williams and Janelle Martinez duet Cardi B's "WAP," which gets a goofy dance going from the crowd that the guys join in on too. I can't help but smile. I drink the rest of my Truly. Bri returns, handing me another one. I crack it open and laugh when Mason twerks against the wall. *Am I having . . . fun? Do I deserve to have fun?*

Bri stands, shaking her hips to the ending of "WAP." "Sing a song with me next, Viv? Please?"

I take another drink, acting like I'm considering it, but

there's no way I can sing. I can't kill my sister, lie to the whole world, and then sing three months later. I should be miserable, atoning for my sins. "I don't know, girl. I'm not really feeling it."

Bri gives me a puppy-dog lip. My stomach swishes with guilt. It would make her night if I gave in, and isn't that why I'm here anyway? To make Bri happy? *I'm here to be a good friend*, I remind myself. I take a long drink and stand. "Fiiiiiiiine. Just one."

Our one song turns into a second, and the room's dancing and singing along so fervently to our off-key pitch, we go into a third, but it's the last one, I swear. While belting out a Doja Cat song, my arm looped around Bri's waist and hers around mine, Riley's death leaves my mind for the first time in months.

I'm singing at the top of my lungs, happy, buzzed tears welling in my eyes, when Phillip Campbell crashes into me while trying to show everyone he can backflip. He smashes my foot, and my toes ignite in pain. I inadvertently yelp, the mic falling from my hands. Out of nowhere, Ash is right beside me.

"Watch where you're going, man!" Ash shoves Phillip away. Ash turns to me. "Are you okay?"

"Yeah." I wiggle my aching toes, making sure nothing's broken.

Phillip puts his hands up and backs away from Ash. "Sorry, no harm meant." He nods at me. The Doja Cat song fades to an end, Bri singing my last line that I missed. The room side-eyes

Ash, who smirks, like he enjoys making people uncomfortable. He reaches into the pocket of his black vest that's covered in sewed-on patches of pentagrams and runes, pulling out a pack of cigarettes.

"Nope, uh-uh," Mason says, snapping his fingers. "Take that outside."

Ash flips him off and struts out the door.

"Eww," a girl mutters. "Why is he here?"

"He literally stinks."

"He wasn't even invited."

"His dad is a *murderer*. Like, move somewhere else already."

I cringe. Oh god, what if people knew I'm a murderer too?

Bri sits on the couch, gesturing for me, and I join her. Someone else starts singing, the room returning to mini concert mode.

"So that was cute, Ash saving you," Bri whispers.

I roll my eyes. "Um, no."

"What if . . ." Bri continues, a conspiratorial tone in her voice, "he's, like, into you? I know he's a freak but hear me out: the town creep and the horror gamer girl. He could be part of your brand."

I scoff. "Not interested. You know, I saw him pick up a dead opossum the other day and put it in his backpack?" The "other day" was last year, but still.

"Eww," Bri says.

Stephanie Williams overhears us. "Wait, what? Ash put a dead opossum in his bag?"

"Yeah." Okay, I might not have seen him put it *in* his backpack, but I definitely saw him pick it up. "He was probably going to do a satanic ritual with it."

Stephanie's eyes widen, and she starts telling the girl next to her about Ash's opossum carcass rituals.

"Fine, not Ash," Bri says. "What about . . . Hector?" Bri raises an eyebrow. "It's been, like, six months since you dumped Tristan. I'm sure there are other guys who aren't just looking for that TAP."

I laugh genuinely for the first time in a while. Tristan was sweet at first, but after the first time we made out, he was all, "Is it true what they say about Asian girls?" I had to google what he meant, and that's when I found out that Asian women are known for having "tight vaginas." Bri and I found it hilarious. Tight Asian Pussy, or TAP, has been one of our inside jokes ever since. But then Tristan got increasingly obsessed with the idea and started telling his friends that even half-Asians have TAP—which was bullshit since one, it's a myth, and two, we never did anything. I dumped him in a glorious TikTok live rant.

"I don't have time for a boyfriend," I tell Bri. "I'm getting my Twitch channel back up." I leave out the part about how I'm too worried that for the rest of my life, any boy I date will only be with me for the TAP.

Around 11:30 p.m., over an hour has passed since the two Trulys I drank, and from articles I've read about how long it takes alcohol to leave your system, I should be good to drive. An underage DUI—or OWI (Operating While under the Influence), as we call them in Iowa, since enough people have gone to prison for drunk-operating a tractor—would not be cool for streamer stardom. I pick up my purse and start eyeing exits, and that's when I notice Tristan at the pool table, laughing with his gross baseball friends. I look away before we make eye contact. I definitely have to get out of here.

What I really want to do is get home and stream *LOCKED IN: An Escape Room Horror Game* while there's still energy left in me. I feel guilty about gaming too, like I shouldn't get to enjoy that while Riley's dead, but if I can revive my channel, if I can make it to the top fifty Twitch streamers, and then someday, the top ten, I'll be able to pay off my parents' mortgage and Dad's business loan. Maybe I'll even buy them a new house, something really nice, something that will make up for all the pain I caused them. If I'm a top streamer, then maybe I can be worthy of getting to live my life while Riley rots in the ground.

I give Bri a hug. "I'm heading out."

"Aww, already?" She pouts, her eyelids heavy from alcohol.

"Yeah."

Her shoulders hang and she groans.

"But I think I'm going to get started with streaming again tonight."

She perks up. "Oh, that's great. I'll try to log in."

I smile and look to Eric, who's drinking water. "Get her home safe."

"Of course." Eric kisses Bri's cheek, and I feel a flicker of envy. Bri's told me that Eric has never fetishized her or made it weird that he has a Black girlfriend or whatever the equivalent of TAP would be. I don't want to be jealous of my best friend, but it's hard to ignore that she claimed one of the only decent guys at our school.

I dart out the side door and cut diagonally across the lawn to my car. In the driver's seat, I open Snapchat. My notifications were turned off all summer, so it's no surprise my DMs are overflowing with unread messages. I haven't posted since early June when I announced that I was taking a hiatus because my little sister had passed. Clearly, people had a lot to say about that, but I don't want to see the responses. I turn on my car's interior light and film myself with a creepy smile filter that also gives me red eyes.

"Hey, guys!" I say to the camera. "I'm back! And I have a new stream for you tonight. It's an indie horror called *LOCKED IN*. We're starting at midnight!" I add the video to my story and cross post to Instagram.

Not even ten seconds pass before I get a like and message

from Robert Murray, aka BobbitWorm on Twitch, my top subscriber and self-proclaimed "number one fan."

I've missed you so much, his message reads. Thank God you're back ♥

It'd be sweet if this guy wasn't . . . forty? fifty? sixty? Who knows, all balding hot-dog skin guys look the same to me from age forty up. I like his message. His bio says he lives in Nevada, so it's not like he's going to show up on my doorstep, and if he wants to throw his money at me, I'll take it.

I load Spotify, figuring I'll continue the same *Crime Junkie* episode I'd started on the way over. But when the app loads, that's not the last thing that was playing. Instead, my phone says I was last listening to Hozier, which I definitely was not. I haven't listened to Hozier in months. I scroll through my "recently played" list. *What the hell?* It's all stuff I used to listen to but have definitely not recently played. Weird. There must've been some glitch or server reset and my app took itself on a trip down memory lane.

I find and resume the *Crime Junkie* episode, then buckle my seat belt, listening to Ashley Flowers describe how one serial killer sewed his victim's eyelids open so she would still look alive. A prickle runs down my neck. I shiver and turn up the heater in my car even though it's 70 degrees out, then reach to put the car in reverse. A sickening knot twists in my stomach, and I'm hit with the sensation that I'm not alone. I whip around to check if someone's in my back seat.

All clear.

Just to be sure, I unbuckle my seat belt and lean all the way back, checking beneath the seats to make sure there isn't a small serial killer scrunched up down there. All good. I turn back to the steering wheel, chuckling. What is up with me? I don't get scared easily. I'm literally *the* horror gamer. Maybe I should take a break from the serial killer podcasts when driving at night.

I turn my headlights on and almost scream. Someone in a black hoodie is standing at the edge of the tree line, staring at me. Their eyes glow a faint orange from beneath a hood, but that must be a reflection on their glasses from the headlights, right? The all-black look means it could be Ash. It's totally his vibe to just stand and stare. I give a wave.

No wave back. Not even a flicker of movement.

Okay, rude.

The figure walks toward me, taking quick, jarring steps, its knees bending too much, its neck kinked to the side. It's moving so fast now it's like it's glitching toward me. *Hell no.* I've played enough horror to know there are two scenarios here: This is just some harmless drunk guy who wants directions, or this is bad, bad news. I throw the car in reverse and hit the gas pedal.

Let's be real—I'm no hero.

THREE MONTHS AGO

For their first real date night since Riley's birth, Mom and Dad were going to see a play in Chicago. Mom said she needed alone time to "reconnect" with Dad, and it would be my job to babysit Riley. Mom wrote a long but reasonable list of all the child safety locks I needed to remember to secure, all the types of food Riley couldn't have, and made me promise not to stream because she knew it was like I entered another realm and could only be summoned back to Earth with a large pepperoni and black olive pizza. I promised her I'd follow the list and stay off Twitch, and I really meant it. Mom and Dad were staying overnight at a hotel in Chicago where I figured the "reconnecting" would happen (shudder), and they'd be back Sunday afternoon.

The whole thing would be around twenty-four hours. I could stay offline that long, and I could certainly keep a toddler alive. I even said those exact words to Mom.

Saturday was a breeze—Riley ate all the carrots with the dinner Mom had prepped and only got a little bit of soap in her eyes at bath time. The only point of stress was my insatiable itch to get on Twitch, like poison ivy meets eczema breakout meets three-day-old sunburn kind of itch. When getting Riley ready for bed, I even found myself turning the routine into a streamer script, and honestly, dressing a toddler is so hard it could be a competitive game.

"We're gonna do it, guys," I said to my imaginary Twitch audience. "This time we're getting her foot in!"

"*Nooo*," Riley screamed, kicking as I tried to pull her legs into the pajama pants.

"She loved these pajamas last night," I said to my pretend audience. "I guess we need a new strategy. Should we check the inventory for different equipment?" I went to the dresser. "Let's see, we have Elvish robes, blessed with a healing enchantment." I held up a white nightgown for Riley and my imaginary Twitch viewers. Riley shook her head, but she had perked up now and stopped crying.

I held up her red onesie with a dinosaur pattern. "What about this dragon plate armor, enchanted with fire resistance?"

"No!"

"What about . . ." I held up her onesie that had a tail and dog ears. "This legendary wolf hide? It grants poison immunity."

Riley let out a high-pitched squeal that meant yes.

"We won!" I announced to my imaginary Twitch audience. "So much grinding, but we did it."

Around 11:00 a.m. on Sunday, Riley and I played Bug Hunt in the backyard. I sat on the grass while Riley teetered around the yard in her frilly blue *Frozen* dress, which she insisted on wearing. She bent down, swiftly capturing roly-polies and lady-bugs with dexterity that didn't seem possible for her chubby hands. When had she become so mobile? I tried to remember when we'd last spent time together aside from dinner, and I could only think of the camping trip last year when Riley was still falling over every three steps and I was climbing trees to get a cell signal. I supposed with how busy I was between Twitch and school (mostly Twitch), I'd missed how fast she was growing up.

"Vivi, look!" Riley said, cradling a particularly large worm.

"Oooh, that's a big one." I snapped a picture of the fat, writhing worm and shared it on my Instagram story.

"Yeah! His name is Daniel."

"Daniel" the worm, I added to my caption.

"You want to find him a girlfriend?" I adjusted the pink butterfly clip holding Riley's side bangs out of her eyes.

"*Yeah!*" She ran back toward the bushes.

I'll spend more time with Riley, I promised myself, though I'd already planned a new permadeath playthrough of *7 Days to Die* and so I knew I probably wouldn't follow through. Still, it was good to at least have the intention.

By the time it was noon, Riley had amassed an army of worm girlfriends for Daniel, and when she tried to eat one, I figured it was time for lunch. I held the sliding glass door open for Riley to go inside, refreshing my Instagram feed. I giggled when Don_the_Hero, another rising Twitch star, replied with a laugh emoji to my story of Daniel the Worm.

In the kitchen, Riley clung to my leg while I made her a

sandwich using the ingredients in the drawer labeled *Riley's Food.* Last year, we learned Riley was allergic to nuts and dairy and fish and wheat and soy, all of which the doctor said she'd likely grow out of, but for the time being, she was high-maintenance AF. I took her food to the living room, then Riley and I sat on the couch to watch *Peppa Pig*, enjoying what would be our last lunch together.

Once I'm home from Mason's party, I rummage through my closet and place my bunny-eared *Bob's Burgers* Louise hat on my desk. It's one of my cute signature novelty looks that will help my fans remember me. I sit in my gaming chair and load *LOCKED IN*, then sign in to Twitch. The Start Streaming button stares back at me. My stomach sinks, guilt twisting through me. The last day I streamed was the day Riley died.

When Mom first told me she was pregnant, I was pissed. I was thirteen and had accepted—even embraced—life as an only child. Who were my parents to think that reproducing at forty was a good idea? They were always lecturing me about not giving in to peer pressure, and here they were, caving in to their baby FOMO. When Riley was born, I politely tolerated this human pupa invading my space, and it was around her first birthday, when she started to walk and use words like "Vivi," that I warmed up to the idea of a little sister.

I open the desk drawer and pick up the Christmas picture of me and Riley from a couple years ago. We're wearing matching green dresses and she's sitting on my lap, her head too big for her body in that goofy-cute proportion one-year-olds have. Riley looks so much like Dad, the same dark eyes and black hair and bulbous nose. I resembled Dad, too, when I was Riley's age. Mom told me that strangers didn't believe I was her baby because I looked nothing like her and looked too Japanese to have a white mother, but around four years old, my cheekbones grew in like Mom's and my mouth took on her fuller shape. I still have the same eyes as Dad: hooded lids and deep brown irises. By the time Riley was two, her eyes had lightened to a gold-flecked hazel like Mom's. I wonder in what other ways Riley would have developed. What would she have looked like at four, at ten, at seventeen? What things would she have liked? *Who would she have been?*

I wipe my eyes, swallowing the lump in my throat. I turn the picture face down and close the drawer. Enough of that. The only way forward is with my Twitch channel. I take off the black beanie I wore to the party and put on my pink bunny-eared hat. *I can do this.* I dab some concealer under my eyes and dust my cheeks with blush to seem less like a dead-inside husk and more like the streamer star I need to be.

"Want a little freedom?" I look over my shoulder to Bakugo.

He's wrapped around a branch, his tongue flicking. I take that as a yes and wheel my chair to his tank, placing him around my neck. His familiar cool touch slows my heart rate and calms my nerves. Dad thinks I'm nuts for referring to Bakugo as my emotional support snake, but it's 100 percent a thing.

I roll back to the computer and turn on my webcam, testing the lighting. I position the lamp so it illuminates my face and the background: a shelf with a dozen Generation 1 Pokémon plushies and the *My Hero Academia*, *Attack on Titan*, and *Full Metal Alchemist* posters hanging on my mint green walls. I straighten my bunny-eared hat. I look cute. Bakugo looks cute. I suck in a big breath.

Three . . . two . . . one.

I hit Start Streaming.

"Hey, hey, hey!" I say as a few viewers begin to trickle in. "It's been a while, I know. Family stuff. But look—we're back with a new game aaaand it's an escape room horror!" I load *LOCKED IN*. I'm surprised by how chipper, how natural, I'm able to sound. I'm really doing this. I click Start New Game. The chat starts up.

where have you been?

omg I missed the snek

what happened?

we thought u died

I thought these questions would trigger me, but when I'm streaming, a whole new persona comes to life. It's how I don't get embarrassed or too self-serious—this isn't really me but a version of myself I've created, like I am an avatar in a game who's also playing a game. Gameception.

"I'll be honest with you guys—my little sister passed away a few months ago." I let out a heavy sigh. "Life just sucks, you know? That's why we game."

totally

irl sucks

why don't we just game 24/7?

all I did was play the Sims when my dad died

I smile and will my eyes not to go misty on-screen. My fans get me.

LOCKED IN loads. My character's standing in the apartment building's first floor, flashlight flickering in her hand. The journal log opens. I read aloud the premise about how I'm a reporter trapped in the building.

"Ready guys?" I say. "You all better have your lights off."

My character's weak flashlight pans across the narrow hallway, illuminating the walls marred with blood and broken fingernails. A message prompts in the upper right-hand corner.

Find Batteries.

I walk my character into the first apartment in the hallway.

I know the batteries are in the bedroom from my first play-through a few hours earlier, but I'll spend some time rummaging around the places I hadn't checked out before.

check the closet

batteries would be in the kitchen drawer duh

can't wait for the jump scares

"Alright guys, checking the closet and then the kitchen." I walk my character up to the closet in the foyer and search the rack of coats. A message appears:

In the pocket of a bloodied trench coat, you find the word 'vermillion' written in fine cursive.

The game logs the note into my *Clues* folder.

what does that word even mean

u don't know? stupid lol

it's a shade of red. lmk if you need any help Viv i'm here

"Let's be nice guys," I say, looking at the usernames. Of course the last comment is from BobbitWorm. "But BobbitWorm is right. It's a pretentious word for red."

Also from BobbitWorm: you're wearing my favorite hat Viv 💘 💘 💘

Eww. I don't react and sort my inventory, then close the window. A pale hand reaches through the closest coats, gripping my character by the throat. Dialogue types across the screen:

Such lovely skin. I want to wear it.

"Nani?!" I say in my best Japanese accent. It's one of the twelve Japanese words I know, all from anime.

runnnn

omae wa mou shindeiru!!!

ok but Viv does have nice skin

she's got that porcelain doll skin

!!!!!!!!!

I mash the spacebar to get away. The hands release me, but then the flashlight goes out, leaving my screen almost completely dark. "Guys, I can barely see!"

CREEPY

try the next room

get the light back on!!

I press the flashlight button a few more times. It comes back on, the light illuminating a mouth full of bloody teeth right against my screen. I shriek and run my avatar into the bedroom.

omg love this game

predictable

i legit just jumped

u speak japanese?? that's cool!

I wish I could speak Japanese. "I'm fluent in anime phrases, but no, I don't actually speak Japanese."

but ur bio says ur japanese?

"Half," I correct. "On my dad's side, and he grew up in the U.S., speaking English. Boring, I know." Dad *can* speak Japanese but doesn't. When I've asked him to teach me, he's said there's no need because "We're American now." Ugh. What does that even mean? I added "half-Japanese" to my bio in the first place because I used to get the dreaded *What are you?* question every stream. The first time a viewer asked me that, I didn't understand, so I stupidly replied, "Umm . . . a gamer?" and then the commenter was all: lol no r u chinese or somethin?

Now I just get asked if I speak Japanese, which I also hate. It reminds me that I'm barely a part of this identity I claim. I would probably seem much more interesting and genuine if I could actually speak Japanese. I've tried using an app to teach myself, but it's too hard. I walk my avatar through the bedroom, searching the dresser and closet before the nightstand, so it doesn't seem like I've played before. After all, I called this a "first-time" stream.

Batteries added to inventory.

I turn around slowly, making sure I aim the camera so my viewers see the creepy crab girl on the ceiling. I wait a moment for her to appear.

wat r u doing

why are you just standing there

She's not here. Weird. Maybe the NPCs react differently on new playthroughs? Seems advanced for a free indie horror. "Sorry guys," I say. "Just planning where to go next."

the room across the hall

upstairs

BASEMENT

"Let's take a vote?" I suggest. The viewers vote in favor of finishing the rest of this floor first, so I enter the room across the hall, the same one where I'd told my secret when I'd been playing earlier. This time, I'll make up some secret about how Bri and I cheated on an exam last year, and when it says I need to tell a "true and darker secret," I'll confess that once in eighth grade, we kissed each other just to practice. The fans will love that candor. BobbitWorm, maybe a little too much.

My character steps into the room. The grandfather clock ticks rhythmically in the corner, and the cloaked NPC is already sitting here on the couch. Bummer. It was creepier how it appeared out of nowhere last time. Its beady glowing eyes stare back at me. I step closer and the NPC stands, slowly stepping toward me, reaching a withering, gray long-nailed hand out.

OMG run

kill it with fire

should've grabbed a weapon!!

The NPC's dialogue appears, but instead of asking for a secret like I expected, the text says:

What is the color of pain?

Huh. That's impressive. The NPCs must have different dialogue programmed for each time you start a new playthrough. Bethesda has less sophisticated mechanics.

"Hmm." I glance up like I need to consider the question. Obviously, the answer must be from that note I found earlier, but the viewers love to feel smart, and I don't mind indulging them.

The chat says: vermillion!!!

"Right, right." I type in the answer. "What would I do without you guys?"

Around 3:30 a.m., viewers start trickling out, leaving just me, BobbitWorm, and a handful of names I don't recognize. Bakugo has moved from my neck to a tight coil around my forearm. I stretch my fingers. My eyes are getting heavy, my quips slow, and after the first floor of *LOCKED IN*, the gameplay is repetitive: open a door, jump scare, find a weird note, answer a question, jump scare.

"I think it's time for bed, guys," I say. "Bakugo needs his beauty rest. Let's pick it up tomorrow?" The chat is slow to respond.

kk

night Viv

idk how I feel about this one, was cool at first but . . .

"Or . . . maybe we should start a new game tomorrow? Or return to a classic? *Silent Hill* throwback?"

new game

BobbitWorm: I'll watch you play anything 🥰

shut up Worm let's go SILENT HILLLLLL

"Alright, guys. I'll figure it out and update you tomorrow. Goodnight." I wave with the arm Bakugo's wrapped around.

I log off, placing Bakugo back in his tank, then collapse onto my bed, smiling into my pillow. *My viewers remember me.* A couple people even resubscribed. It really is going to be okay.

I have the nightmare I always have about Riley. I'm running for her, but the hallway is getting longer, and I'm sinking through the floor, the carpet liquifying beneath me, siphoning my body into the ground, filling my lungs. My chest burns with the need for air. I claw at my throat, Riley's shrill, feral screams echoing in my ears.

My eyes flitter open, my heart pounding. Slowly, the shock from the nightmare wears off. I close my eyes again.

"Vivi," a child's voice whispers.

My eyes snap open. *Vivi?* No one calls me that. No one other than Riley. I must still be dreaming.

"Vivi," the voice says again, more urgently. I move my hand to pinch myself awake, but my arm won't move. I try to move my legs to stand, but they don't respond. *What the hell?* My throat tightens.

I turn my head, but that's immobilized, too, like I'm encased in concrete. My mouth turns cottony; my heart is beating so hard I can feel blood pulse in my neck. All I can move are my eyes.

The room is dimly lit by the power button on my desktop, still glowing while idle. Something rustles in the corner by the closet. I can only stare at the ceiling. A shadow appears above me, the shape of a head and shoulders. The shadow steps closer.

I try to say, "Who's there?" but my mouth is immobilized. All that comes out is a whimper. Saliva starts to build up in my mouth, pooling in the back of my throat. I try to swallow but can't. Drool leaks at the corners of my lips. A coldness seeps through the room; goosebumps erupt over my arms.

Over the sound of the fan, I can make out a faint, raspy breathing. It's close and getting closer. *Shit.* My eyes dart around. The shadow on the ceiling towers over me. The raspy breathing quickens right next to my face, the breath cold and sour.

A freezing hand grips my forearm and squeezes painfully. My skin gives way, sharp nails digging into my flesh. Warm blood trickles down my arm. I try to scream, but my lips won't part. Tears sting my eyes.

The hand lets go. My forearm throbs.

A quiet voice speaks in my ear, the words so low, so faint, I thought I misheard. But after replaying it again and again in my mind, I know what it said.

"Such lovely skin."

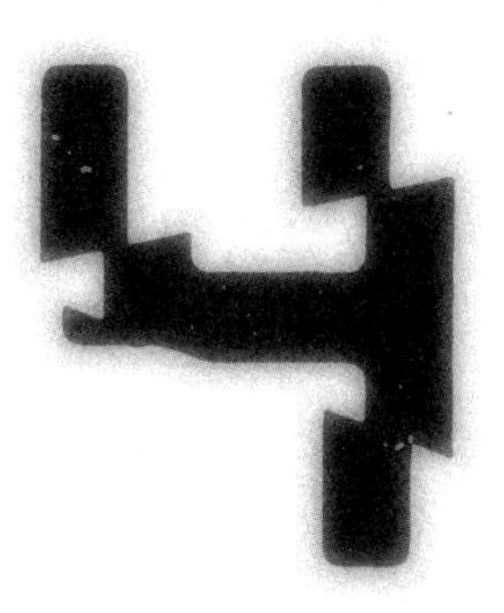

On Monday morning, I lean against the bathroom counter, blending concealer under my eyes, then I stand back to look at myself in the mirror. Brushed and straightened, my green-gray hair isn't *that* bad. With my cat-eye black eyeliner, the whole look gives off a punk vibe, which I don't totally hate.

Mom walks by, dressed in her work-from-home cardigan and stretchy slacks, her shoulder-length light brown hair freshly blow-dried. She pauses in the doorway. "You're sure you're ready to go back to school?"

I zip up my makeup bag. "Yeah, I think so." I can't help but notice that Mom's green cardigan is new, and it doesn't have buttons like the ones she used to wear. We've been a button-free household since Riley's death. My stomach aches with guilt.

Mom steps closer to me, smiling softly. "Just know that it's okay if you need more time. Or if you change your mind and realize it's too much." She stares at me, her hazel eyes intense, and they look so much like Riley's, I have to look away. I'm grateful more than ever that I have Dad's eyes, so I don't see Riley when I look in the mirror. I couldn't stand that.

"You and Dad didn't take much time off before going back to work."

"We didn't have a choice, honey. Someone has to pay the bills."

I flinch, remembering how much the funeral cost, the jobs that Dad lost from taking a few weeks off. "I'll be eighteen in, like, ten months." Really, Riley's death makes me feel like I aged to forty overnight, and this sort of tragedy seems like it should qualify one to auto age up to adulthood, but I don't say any of this to Mom.

"I'm glad you're going back to school," Mom says. "I was hoping you'd get to have a normal senior year." She pauses. "I just don't want you to feel pressured to do it for us."

I swallow the lump forming in my throat. I hate that Mom doesn't get to just grieve Riley but also has to worry about how this whole thing affects me too. "Mom, stop—you're going to make me cry my eyeliner away."

Mom smiles. "You don't need it anyway, but okay. I'll stop."

I turn back to the mirror, finishing my brow liner.

"Did you put on sunscreen too?"

"No. I'll be outside for, like, ten minutes today."

"You've been inside all summer." She puts her hand on my cheek, turning my face toward hers. "You're lucky you have your dad's genes. Take care of your skin, okay? You'll look young forever. Look at me." She gestures at her neck, pulling on the thin, stretchy skin. "I already need a neck lift."

"Yeah, yeah, yeah." It's not the first time I've heard all this about my "nice skin," but it never gets less annoying.

Mom points to the sunscreen on the shelf. "Put it on, okay?"

"I will in a minute, promise." I am not putting it on.

She turns to leave, then pauses. "You're not still having nightmares, right?"

"No."

She stares at the poorly concealed bags under my eyes. "You sure?"

I hold Mom's gaze. She's so skilled with makeup, it's hard to notice, but now I see the dark circles under her own eyes, the puffiness of her eyelids. I can't cause her any more stress, any more pain, so I do what I'm best at: I lie.

"Maybe I didn't sleep the best these last couple nights, but it's just anxiety about school." I leave out the part about how Saturday night I had the worst sleep paralysis of my life. The nightmare was so visceral, I was almost convinced it was real, and I was so paranoid about it happening again, I barely slept at all last night.

"Dad picked up more of that white chocolate creamer you like, if you want to take some coffee with you."

"Thanks, Mom."

"Sunscreen!" She walks down the hall.

I wait until I can't hear her steps anymore. The last thing she needs to know is that I'm not just having nightmares but a full-on psychosomatic reaction. I've been trying not to think about it, but the night of my sleep paralysis, I must've freaking clawed myself. I wince as I roll up my sleeve just to check, and yep, it's still there.

In the center of my forearm are five scabbed puncture wounds.

In third period, I sit with my chin resting on my fist, lazily taking notes with my other hand. Ms. Newman drones on about the symbolism we need to be close reading for when we start *The Handmaid's Tale*. So far, the day hasn't been bad at all. The teachers are sweet and give me distance. No one has called on me. There have been a few looks, but going to Mason's party helped break the ice of my return to society.

I rest my eyes for a moment, the gentle patter of the rain on the window lulling me to sleep. Bri has AP Poli Sci this period instead of Dystopian Lit, so she's not here to keep me entertained. I open my eyes to write another sentence, then close them again. It'd be so easy to nap like this, and maybe I will. Just for a minute.

I jolt upright as my head starts to fall forward. I pretend I'm stretching my neck like that didn't just happen. But something feels off, like I'm stuck in a dream. My eyes can't focus, as if I'm looking at the room through a fishbowl. Great. I'm having a bout of dissociative brain fog and I'm pretty sure Ms. Newman is staring right at me, but I can't tell for sure. The hairs on my arms and neck rise. I shiver even though I'm wearing a sweatshirt. Nausea bubbles in my gut. Am I coming down with something?

I start to raise my hand to ask if I can go to the bathroom, and that's when I see it—someone through the window, standing in the shade of the tree on the lawn. Watching me. They're dressed in all black, a big hood pulled over their head. For some reason, I can see this person clearly even though everything else feels blurred. Their head tilts upward, revealing small glowing eyes. A chill runs across my skin, the thought hitting me that this is the same thing that came to me in my nightmare. But that's insane. That was just a dream. This is something real—it looks like the same person I saw when I was leaving Mason's party. A stalker.

All I want is to see their face, but from where I'm looking, it's like they don't have one, just two freaking weird eyes. It has to be the way the hood is shading their features, but still, their facelessness bothers me. I glance around to see if anyone else is noticing this person standing outside like a total creep, but everyone has their heads in their notebooks.

I stand and quickly walk to the teacher's desk. "Ms. Newman, can I use the restroom?"

"Sure." She opens the drawer and hands me the pass. I grab it, still watching the figure outside, which hasn't moved at all. "You okay?" Ms. Newman asks, her blue eyes filled with concern.

"Yeah, fine. Had a lot of coffee. Stomach hurts." I rush out of the room and hurry down the hall. If my stalker has at least a few points in intelligence, they'll have left before I make it, especially if they are in fact stalking me—but if I'm quick, I can hopefully identify them. I'm practically sprinting down the stairs, but when I make it outside—they're gone. *Damn it.*

There is something here that might be useful though: footprints in the mud right where I'd seen my stalker standing. Someone was definitely here. Who would be stalking me? Maybe Ash, since Bri planted it in my brain that he's into me. Or worse, what if it's some rabid fan? An incel twenty-year-old troll? Or some old guy, like BobbitWorm?

I lean closer to the footprint, putting my shoe next to it. What's weird is that all those people would probably have bigger feet than me. These footprints are the exact same size as mine.

After school, Bri and I study together at her place, sitting at the long wooden table in the den, the portable speaker playing lo-fi beats. We take notes for fifteen minutes, then quiz each other with flashcards. At the end of every half hour, we play one *Magic: The Gathering Arena* match with a goal to secure a win in five minutes or less.

I hold up a biology flashcard for Bri.

"Goddamn it." She throws her head back and groans when she misses step four out of the one thousand citric acid cycle steps.

"You weren't that far off." I turn the card around to show her the answer.

Bri folds her arms. "But that's not good enough for Mr. Holmes. I need an A if I want Dartmouth to even look at me."

"I know, I know." I glance at the time. "Twelve minutes till our next *Magic* game. Let's go over the digestive system? Then we'll try good old citric acid cycle again."

Bri nods and shows me a card about the common bile duct's path. I don't give a crap about Mr. Holmes's biology test or college. But Bri has twenty universities ranging from state schools to Ivy Leagues with all their pros and cons organized in a spreadsheet. Our counselor told us to go to college with an open major and explore options, but Bri's been dead set on becoming a lawyer since freshman year. Her spreadsheet even includes each school's undergraduate success rate with getting into top law programs. I know how much studying means to her, so I dig up some vague memory about the common bile duct taking bile from the gallbladder to the duodenum, and I get it right. Bri cheers.

At 4:30 p.m., we log into *Magic: Arena* and start a historical brawl game. Bri's Blue control deck versus my Red and Black aggro.

Discord dings with a message as my first dragon enters the battlefield.

BobbitWorm: aww playing Magic but no stream? that's not fair :(

I roll my eyes and exit the message.

"Who is it?" Bri asks.

"BobbitWorm."

"*Eww.* Still? Does he have no life?"

I shrug. Bri's about to use her Thassa, Deep-Dwelling to blink her Dream Eater and send all my dragons back to my hand, but before she can, I shout, "You forgot about my trap card!" in my best *Yu-Gi-Oh!* impression and exile her Dream Eater.

"Oh goddamn it." Bri groans. "I even had a counterspell, but I tapped out."

I attack, killing her off with my Lathliss, Dragon Queen and all her dragon minions. "Damn, I wish we'd streamed that match. It was such a good win!"

"One more quick game?" Bri asks.

"Cuz I beat you so easily?" I smirk, but I'm surprised. Normally, Bri's eager to get back to homework, and I'm the one who wants to play longer. I load the new match.

She snickers. "No. It's just nice getting to hang out like this again."

"Ugh. I know. I'm sorry I was so absent this summer."

"I don't mean that. You needed to grieve, like totally understandable. I mean even before this summer." Bri summons her first creature. "You were always so busy on Twitch, and don't get me wrong, I support your ambitions. Like, yes, please be a girlboss streamer star, but remember in middle school when we'd play *Stardew Valley* and it wasn't about entertaining your subscribers; it was . . . just for fun?"

I pause, digging up a faint memory of me and Bri lying side by side on our stomachs on my bedroom floor, sowing crops and upgrading our farm on our laptops. I'm hit with a strange longing nostalgia for the times when Bri and I would stay up all night gaming together. But now Riley's dead because of me, and I don't *get* to game for fun anymore. I *have* to. It's the only way to make things better.

"Yeah . . . those were the good times," I deflect. Bri summons a planeswalker and I don't stop her even though I have a counterspell.

Discord dings again.

BobbitWorm: I bet you're winning huh? ;)

Me: yah but dude I'm 17, chill on the hearts and winky faces k?

BobbitWorm: :(((

"You're not responding to that old guy, right?" Bri says. "That'll just encourage him. You need to ghost his ass."

"I just told him to stop being a creep."

Bri rolls her eyes. She attacks me with a swarm of soldiers and kills me with a satisfied smirk. "Let's play more *Magic* this weekend? And what did you think about the new release I sent you? We can draft, like old times. You're free right?"

"Huh?"

Bri gives me an exasperated look. "I sent the new *Magic* set to you on Instagram last night. It says you left me on read, so I figured we'd talk about it when we hung out today?"

"I don't remember that. . . ." I unlock my phone.

Bri flips open her color-coded planner. "Well, I want to know if we're going to draft so I can write it into my schedule."

What is she talking about? Did I open her message while half-asleep and forget about it? I open my Instagram DMs. There is a message from Bri that's read, one that I don't remember reading at all. My stomach drops when I see the messages above it. They're from the night of Mason's party, a response to a selfie I put of us on my story.

Brianna: we look hot!!! soooo good to see you tonight girl!!! glad you came through

Me: sorry i left a little early!! i had fun and am glad i sucked it up!!

The words are true and exactly what I would've said.

The problem is—I never sent them.

I really do have a stalker, one who's hacked my accounts. No thank you. I spend the rest of our study session changing all my passwords.

"I'm so creeped out that someone messaged me as you." Bri shudders.

"Umm, *you're* creeped out? How do you think I feel?!"

"I'd be losing my shit if I were you. Who do you think it is?" Her face contorts like something stinks. "Is it that old BobbitWorm guy who's obsessed with you?"

"But why would he message you? It doesn't make any sense. And he's a boomer—how would he even know how to hack into my account?"

"Oh my god," Bri says, a lightbulb practically popping up above her head. "What if it's Ash? What if he wanted to pretend to be you to see if we'd talked about him? Because he's totally in love with you but doesn't know how to express it with his little goth heart. He gives me major stalker vibes."

I snort. "That's way too convoluted of a plan for something like a crush."

"Okay, but remember at sixth grade camp, when they found him creeping by the girls' cabins and he said he 'got lost on the way to the restroom'?" Bri sits back, folding her arms in her confident *I'm right* pose. "He was starting to pick out victims then."

"How do you remember that after all these years?" I'd honestly forgotten about it.

"Because he was outside *my* cabin! I don't trust him."

I have to admit, if it is Ash, then that makes the whole thing way less scary. It's just a teen boy I can handle, not some psycho old man with a van stocked with rope and duct tape. All the *Crime Junkie* episodes about internet stalkers come flooding into my mind. "But what if . . ." I start, sucking air between my teeth, "it's not Ash, and it is BobbitWorm because he's, like, secretly a tech genius, or it's any other scary old guy on the internet who's obsessed with my streamer persona?" My parents are always worried about that, and now I hate to admit they might be right.

Bri nods slowly. "Yeah, honestly, we should report it. I can take us to the police station right now."

I hesitate, thinking of the times I've walked in on Dad crying in the laundry room only for him to pretend he was just looking for something. Mom's sobs she thinks I can't hear over the sound of the shower. They're miserable because of me. I can't burden them with this too. "I'm changing my passwords, so it might not even be an issue anymore."

"But these kinds of things escalate." Bri gives me wide eyes.

She might be right, but Mom and Dad are so fragile right now, if I stress them out about me having a potential stalker, they might shatter. They might even lock me down in an overprotective attempt to keep me safe. I can't let some stalker dictate my life like that.

Once I'm home, I clear all cookies and caches on my desktop and iPad. I must've logged in to a phishing link at some point. How could I have been so careless? After I finish resetting every password on my computer, I change out of my clothes, itching the scabs from the scratch on my arm. The skin surrounding the scabs is veiny and yellowing. Gross. Is it infected? If Mom and Dad didn't have enough on their plate already, I might ask if they think it warrants a trip to urgent care, but considering that I've already caused enough problems, a thorough wash and a coat of Neosporin should be enough. I'll make sure not to swim in any lakes until it's healed.

I go to my closet to change out of my jeans and into something more comfortable, but when I slide open the door, my eyes narrow in suspicion. Something looks different. I'm not sure what, but after a minute of rummaging around, I realize my purple *MST3K* hoodie is missing, a few of my hats—including the Louise one—and my pair of Converse. WTF.

My journals have been moved, too, and one is propped open. My pulse starts to climb. Did my stalker break into my room? *No.* Mom was probably looking for some of her clothes I'd borrowed and forgot to return. But then why were all the missing things stuff that I wear regularly, and why are my journals open? Good thing I never wrote a word about Riley's death—the journals are just ramblings about my insecurities over my Twitch image, the whole breakup with Tristan, and my jealousy over Eric and Bri's happily-ever-after. Boring, really.

I run downstairs and to the laundry room in case Mom brought my clothes here. I search the dryer and shelves, but there's nothing. Shit. *Okay, think.* Maybe I really did misplace my things. Maybe I rummaged through the closet and threw the shoes under the bed and just don't remember doing so. But if that's not the case, then that means what I feared must be true.

I text Bri: some of my clothes are missing. maybe they're just lost somewhere around the house or . . .

Brianna: or what?? you think someone stole your clothes???? your stalker?!?!

Me: idk maybe???

Brianna: ok let me think

Brianna: if it's the stalker then it's probably not BobbitWorm since he doesn't even live here . . . unless he came to town?!!

My stomach backflips. I remember BobbitWorm saying that the Louise hat is his favorite. There's no way he'd go that far though, right?

Brianna: or it's Ash

Brianna: i bet Ash totally has a shrine of you. and I'm not trying to be funny. you should go to the cops before he kidnaps you

I groan and text back: i need to search my room one more time. and no cops. my parents would not be ok.

Obviously Bri's really on one with this whole Ash thing, but now that I'm thinking about it, might she be right? I remember how he'd acted defensive of me at the party when Phillip had accidentally smashed my foot. Maybe Ash was a little too defensive? Maybe he has a creepy fetish like Tristan? And someone dressed in all black has definitely been watching me. All black is 100 percent Ash's look.

I head back toward my room.

"Hey, kiddo!" Dad says, filling a glass of water at the kitchen sink. Beside him, Mom slices a kiwi.

"Hey, Dad."

"How was the first day back?" Dad takes off his Ken's HVAC Installation and Repair work hat, exposing his balding head.

"Fine. Mom, you didn't go into my closet at all, did you?"

She pauses slicing and looks at me. "No. Why?"

"Just wondering."

"You okay?" Dad asks, chuckling. "Did anyone give you any trouble today? You need me to come rough up anyone at school?" Dad chuckles again and I force a smile for him. He never used to be a chuckler, but ever since Riley's death, he's nonstop with the chuckles. It's probably the only thing keeping him from bursting into sobs.

"Nope," I say. "It was all good."

Mom puts a row of sliced kiwi on a plate and slides it toward me. "Here, sit down. Have a snack."

"I'm kind of in the middle of something." I impatiently shift my weight side to side.

"Streaming again?" Dad asks, an edge of concern in his voice.

"Yeah."

Mom and Dad give each other a knowing glance.

"Look, I'm glad you're getting back to normal," Dad starts, "after . . ."

"Uh-huh. Yeah, it's going well." *Please don't talk about Riley.* I can't stand hearing them say her name, the pain it brings to their faces.

Dad squeezes my shoulder. "But don't let this little hobby take over your life, okay?" Another chuckle. "College is just around the corner. You've got to start thinking about the real world, not waste all your time in video games."

Oh god. Not a lecture. "Yeah, don't worry. Bri and I already had a biology study session today so it's all good."

"Then you know how important it is to get your vitamins." Mom gestures at the plate of fruit. "I'm not letting you get on that computer without eating something healthy. Remember when the doctor said you were malnourished and Vitamin D deficient? You forget to eat when you're streaming those games."

"Ugh, that was in winter, Mom. Like, everyone's Vitamin D deficient in winter." I stuff the kiwi into my mouth, chewing quickly. Sure, maybe I'd gone a few days in a Twitch subathon during which I sustained myself with only Nutri-Grain bars and after which I felt inexplicably weak and achy and Mom insisted we go to the doctor. But that was one time. I drink lots of milk now, so I'm fine.

I swallow the last of the kiwi, and Mom gives me a satisfied nod.

In my room, I check the closet again, more thoroughly this time, and go through each dresser drawer. My hat, sweatshirts, and shoes are still missing. I kneel beside my bed. A rancid, burnt smell assaults my nose. What the hell is that? Rotten food? I flip the bed skirt up but it's too dark to see anything. I grab my phone to use the flashlight.

Something rustles. There's a *creak* followed by a few rapid snaps, like the sound of knuckles cracking. Did an animal get in here? I shine my phone's flashlight under the bed. My blood turns cold, my stomach knotting. There's a body. Its knees are jammed up by its neck, head cocked way too far to the side, skin brown and rotting, pieces of flesh dangling off the elbows and knees. Fear roots me to the ground. Small orange eyes open; the pupils are black reptilian slits. Before I can scream, the body scutters forward like a spider, sharp-angled limbs moving inhumanly fast. I leap backward, crashing into the closet doors. I scramble upright and run down the stairs, screaming, "Something's in my room!"

"Viv, what's wrong?" Mom asks, eyes wide.

"Evil dead guy!" I scream. "Under the bed!"

Mom and Dad bolt up the stairs.

"You saw *what* under the bed?" Mom asks, stepping into my room.

"A monster—I don't know! Just check." I gnaw on my fingernails.

Dad whips up the bed skirt, shining his phone light under. Nothing—of course. Just old socks, hair ties, and Fiber One bar wrappers.

I press my fingers to my face. It was there a minute ago. I swear it was there. *Or am I going insane because why would there be a dead guy under my bed?*

"You're sure you saw something?" Dad stands.

I nod, my back pressed against the wall.

Mom frowns, eyebrows knitting together. "Maybe it was too

early to go back to school. Why don't you stay home the rest of this week—"

"No. This has nothing to do with that." I gesture at the bed. "I swear—" I pause. Clearly, nothing is under there. Insisting there was just makes me sound nuts. Mom will put me in a padded room if I keep harping on like this. "I don't know. Thanks for checking. Maybe it's just the horror games getting to me."

Dad stares at me, his face filled with scrutinizing concern. "You sure you're okay? You can talk to us, Viv. You don't have to make up stories for us to listen—"

My stomach wallops. He thinks this is like the time I pretended to break my arm. Bri broke her arm and got showered with gifts and got to stay home with her mom for a week, and so I pretended to break mine, too, so I could have a week at home with my parents. I was twelve. "This isn't like that, Dad! I'm fine, I swear."

"Maybe you should try playing something nice once in a while," Mom says. "Not so gory and dark."

"Uh-huh."

"And really Viv, clean up those wrappers and dirty clothes." Mom glances at the trash under the bed, then she and Dad leave the room.

I sit on my computer chair. I'm not getting anywhere near that bed right now. What the hell is going on? Maybe the stress over this stalker situation is getting to me, and I'm not exactly well rested. Maybe I'm seeing things. But the thing under the bed sounded, looked—even smelled—so real.

My phone vibrates in a few rapid successions. It's on the floor by the closet where I'd thrown it when I leapt back. I walk over and pick it up.

Brianna: girl, look!!!!!! LOOK

She sends a screenshot of Ash's Instagram story: He's playing guitar in a dark room, his hair shrouding his face. Bri's circled something pink in the background.

Brianna: that's your hat!!!

I zoom in to see the exact same bunny ears of my missing *Bob's Burgers* hat.

I get into my car, the shakes from my under-the-bed jump scare wearing off. *You imagined the whole thing*, I tell myself, pulling out of the driveway. *You're just dipping your toes into horror games again, and that plus the stalker situation and the terrible things you did this summer have you all screwed up. But now you know who the stalker is, and you're going to put that little creep in his place!* I turn up the radio and drive down the road toward Ash's place.

Back when Dad was just a contractor before he had his own HVAC business, we lived in the building across the street from Ash's apartment. I remember the cops lining the street when they'd tracked Ash's dad's car home after the hit and run. Mom had wept all day for those two poor nurses. Dad said Ash's father deserved to get locked up and the key thrown away.

I park next to Ash's rusted 2001 Chevy Metro. It's the only car in town with pentagram stickers. A faded bumper sticker reads POWERED BY SATAN. I'd probably find that funny if I wasn't so pissed. I get out of my car, slamming the door behind me. I'm ready to kick in Ash's door and tell him to leave me the hell alone. The problem is there are at least thirty apartment units here and I don't know which one Ash lives in, but a quick search on usphonebook.com tells me it's apartment 11. Two can play this stalker game.

I pound on his door. *What the hell was he thinking, taking my stuff? That I wouldn't find out and stand up for myself?* I pound harder. Shit. What if his mom is sleeping? It's only 5:00 p.m., but if she's still a flight attendant, she probably has odd working hours. Or worse, what if usphonebook.com was wrong, and this isn't the right apartment? I peer through the crack in the blinds and see the same guitar from his Instagram propped against the couch. This is totally Ash's place. I knock again, but gentler. *Stay calm.* It's just a hat. And a sweatshirt. And a pair of shoes. And the fact that *he went into my house.*

All my rage comes roiling back, and I bang harder on the door.

The door whips open. Ash's long sandy-blond hair is tousled like he'd been napping, a pair of over-the-ear headphones looped around his neck. He stares back at me, eyes wide and eyebrows raised like *I'm* the crazy one.

"What are you doing?" he asks.

"Coming to get my shit back from you! Who do you think you are, stealing from me?"

"What shit?" His eyes narrow and he widens his arms so he's blocking the doorway.

"My clothes are missing, and I saw *this* on your Instagram story!" I whip out my phone and pull up the screenshot. "That's my hat!"

Ash scoffs. "I have no idea what you're talking about." He side-eyes the picture. "You think I stole something from you? Why would I even do that?" He steps back, gesturing for me to come in. "Come investigate. Go ahead and film it if you want. You TikTok lackeys are so full of yourselves."

"Excuse me? I'm a Twitch streamer." I shove past him into the apartment. "Where's your room?"

He points to the door closest to the kitchen. It occurs to me that if Ash is, in fact, stalking me, then maybe it's not the smartest idea to plant myself right in his room. But before Riley's death, I joined Mom at her CrossFit gym. Ash is so stringy I doubt he's ever done a squat in his life. I can put up a good fight, but just to be safe, I'll position myself near the door in case I need to bolt.

I walk into his room—it's more of a dark cave than a

bedroom: the windows shielded with blackout curtains; the walls covered in Slayer, Korn, and Nine Inch Nails posters; the air warm and humid; the floor littered with clothes, Reese's wrappers, and bones—but from KFC chicken and not dead opossums.

"So? Where's my stuff?" I snap. "My hat?" I point again to the screenshot Bri took of him.

Ash looks at the picture so bewildered, my face reddens. If this is a mistake, then I totally seem insane.

He walks past me into the room, yanking a stuffed animal off the shelf. He shoves it in my face. "Here you go," he says, sarcastically. "Happy?"

I look at the picture, then back at the pink stuffed rabbit he's holding in my face. *Crap.* "Well—" I stammer, my face burning. "You still hacked into my Instagram account!"

"Are you high?" Ash asks, so baffled my confidence plummets. "You know what—I wish I thought to do something like that, but it's so dumb and petty it never even crossed my mind." He snickers. "Besides, everyone already thinks I'm fucked up, so really, what would I even gain by denying it? If I 'hacked your accounts,' I'd be bragging about it." He folds his arms and holds my gaze, glaring at me. I don't detect any lies.

Shit.

I sit on his bed, burying my face in my hands. I'm such an asshole, but more than that, if Ash isn't taking my stuff, if he's not the one logging in to my accounts, then who the hell is? BobbitWorm? My hands start to tremble, a chill shuddering across my skin. This was way less scary when it was just a creepy teen boy I knew and could handle.

"This was stupid. I'm sorry," I stammer, tears welling in my eyes. I can't believe I'm crying, but I've only been back in society a couple days, and I've already screwed it up. Royally.

"Hey, come on." Ash's voice softens. "I shouldn't have snapped at you. I know you have a lot going on with . . ."

"My dead sister?" I look up at him. "That's not the problem," I say, even though it is always my problem. "It's more than that. Someone's stalking me. They hacked my Instagram. I saw them outside class the other day. They took my shoes!" I stifle an ugly sob. I almost mention the dead guy I saw under my bed, but I don't want to come off as even more crazy than I already sound.

"Whoa . . ." Ash glances around uncomfortably, like he doesn't know what to do about this crying girl on his bed. "That's . . . scary."

I wipe my face. "I'm fine." I take a deep breath, my voice steadying. "I just need to figure this out before it, you know, escalates."

"Have you tried tracing where the log-ins are from?"

I shake my head. It seems so obvious now to have tried that first, but I never even got any notification that my accounts had been logged in to from a different device. I pull out my phone and look at the log-in activity under my security settings. The results make my stomach queasy.

The map icon points to my house. It hasn't been logged in to from any other locations.

I hold up my phone to show Ash. "It doesn't show any other location info. Whoever's doing this—it's untraceable." BobbitWorm couldn't pull that off, right? *Or they're logging in from my room.* But that's impossible.

Ash plops down on his computer chair. "Hmm. What else was taken from your room?"

"My sweatshirt. My journals were open like someone read them." I shudder. I hadn't thought much of it at the time, but now, that detail is so creepy.

"Your journals?" Ash cocks an eyebrow. "You're sure this isn't just some jealous boyfriend snooping through your stuff?"

"No! I don't have a boyfriend." I groan, realizing that this whole thing probably sounds so dumb and petty. "I should go." I stand, rubbing the itching scab on my arm. "Just forget about this whole thing."

"It's alright." Ash stands too, sweeping his hair out of his face. "Look, I get it if you don't want to drag the cops into it, so if you need help, hit me up, okay?" Ash tells me his number and I enter it into my phone.

"Thanks," I say, genuinely, and I'm surprised. I've always heard, and said myself, that Ash is an unhinged lunatic. Last year,

Bri and I made a poll ranking our classmates from everything from hottest to dumbest to most-likely-to-shoot-up-the-school. I listed Ash as the number one nominee for that last one, and everyone in the Snapchat poll agreed. But was I wrong?

"No problem," he mumbles toward the floor.

"I'm sorry I was such a dickhead. It wasn't cool accusing you of—"

"Don't worry about it." Ash waves his hand like it was nothing. "All's forgiven."

I'm surprised he's getting over it so easily. I probably wouldn't forgive him that quickly if he was the one who burst into my place accusing me of things I didn't do. In fact, I'd probably call the cops on him. I roll up my sleeve and scratch the scabs on my arm. "Well, I'll see you around."

Ash's face turns pale when he sees my scabs, his eyes widening. "Uhhh, how did you get that?"

I pull my sleeve back down. "Just a scratch. Why?"

"The pattern of the scratches—it looks like it might be umm . . . Nah, you'll just think I'm nuts," he mutters. "You better go before my mom gets home."

He walks me to the door, his brown eyes swimming with concern.

THREE MONTHS AGO

Halfway through Riley's gluten-free, dairy-free, extra-bland, and extra-safe sandwich, she dropped a chunk of crust between the couch cushions.

"Make sure you pick that up," I said.

Riley giggled and mashed the bread farther down into the cushions. Really? Ugh, toddlers were so annoying.

I pulled the cushions apart, exposing a row of bread crusts Riley must've shoved down here before, pieces of wrappers, and a quarter-sized brown button from one of Mom's cardigans. I picked the button up and put it in my pocket. She'd been looking for that and was worried about it being a choking hazard along with a dozen other random things in the house: the batteries in the TV remote (securely taped shut), the Tide pods (switched to liquid detergent), grapes (permabanned).

Two *Peppa Pig* episodes later, Riley leaned against me, eyes closed, mouth open, a puddle of drool forming in her bottom lip. I propped her against the pillow and lowered the volume of the TV.

My phone vibrated.

Mom: How are my girls?

Me: Good!

Mom: We're getting lunch, then we'll head back in time to beat the traffic

Me: Ok!

I scrolled through TikTok, liking Bri's new SpongeBob meme. I kept scrolling and stopped on the newest TikTok from GinnySnow—aka my nemesis. She was dancing in front of the camera in zombie makeup and a bloodied nurse costume, the caption: Subathon tomorrow! We're going twelve hours straight in 7 Days to Die permadeath mode—if I die, we add another hour to the subathon. Ready???

I groaned. What the hell? Was she blatantly stealing my ideas now? Sure, I occasionally piggybacked off her ideas, but I at least waited a little while. Like when she played *Tetris* blindfolded, I waited a month before doing it too. I'd literally *just* announced an upcoming permadeath *7 Days to Die* stream. *I should beat her to it. I should go log in and play right now.*

I stood and took a few steps toward the stairs. I glanced back at Riley, making sure she was sound asleep. Her hands were tucked under her chin, eyelids fluttering as she dreamed. What would the harm be if I went upstairs and streamed *7 Days to Die* for twenty minutes or so? I could just spawn a world and character to get viewers interested. A teaser.

Riley let out a snore that was comically loud for her small body. *No. I can't do it. Mom and Dad will be home soon. Just wait. What's a few more hours?*

I went back to the couch, sitting down so forcefully I woke Riley, and it wasn't an accident. If she was awake, if she needed me to keep her entertained, I'd be less likely to ditch her and go get on Twitch.

She blinked at me with sleepy, heavy eyelids.

"Mom won't be happy if you nap too much and aren't tired for bedtime," I said. "So, what do you want to do now?"

She thought for a moment, then immediately perked up. "I want dessert!"

On my way home from Ash's, I stop at the pet store to get frozen mice and fresh bedding for Bakugo, buying only the best for my son. Even another reason to get my Twitch channel thriving again: Bakugo doesn't eat often, but when he does, it's pricey.

When I get home, there are two empty pizza boxes and three dirty dinner plates on the table. Weird. Did Mom and Dad have a guest over? I put the boxes in the recycling and the plates in the dishwasher. Mom used to be a neat freak, but ever since Riley died, she's been relying on me to clean up more. And I don't mind. It's the least I can do. Once the table's clean, I go upstairs to my room. My mouth hangs open when I see what's on my bed.

It's my missing purple sweatshirt—not missing anymore. It's folded and on my bed. Is someone messing with me? Because, hand to god, this was *not* here when I left. I pick it up and inspect it, searching for some clue. A note. A suspicious hair. But there's nothing on the sweatshirt other than a speckle of pizza sauce I don't remember eating. I'm hit with a stab of paranoia. I grab my reading lamp with my right hand, holding it up like a weapon, and flip open the bed skirt. Nothing's there. No creepy dead guy. I really was seeing things.

Still, this sweatshirt thing is so weird. My hand twitches to text Ash and tell him that my sweatshirt is somehow magically back, but we basically just had our first real conversation since elementary school. Why is he the one I want to talk to about this? I start typing all this out to Bri in a text, but what if she thinks I'm nuts? Maybe I am. I look at the sweatshirt. Did I leave it on the bed and completely overlook it? No. I swear it wasn't here before I left. But I haven't been sleeping well. What if I'm imagining all this weirdness and creating my own panic?

Dad walks by my room. "Hey, Viv."

"Hi, Dad." I glance away from my phone to look at him. His graying hair looks thinner than ever, his hooded eyes heavy with fatigue. "How's work?" I ask. "You're not taking it too hard, right?" I feel a pang of guilt realizing I haven't asked Dad about his business in a while.

Dad's face softens. "It's always hard. But I'm an old man.

Tough work is what we do. That's why you're going to college, so you can get a good job."

"Right. . . ."

"So," Dad chuckles, "I'm surprised you decided to try green olives with your pizza tonight."

Whoa whoa whoa. I wouldn't touch a green olive with a ten-foot pole. What is he talking about? I wasn't even at dinner. "Dad, what are you talking about? I definitely did not eat green olive pizza."

Dad frowns. "I could've sworn you did." He takes another step into my room, folding his arms. "Look, I want to finish our conversation from earlier."

"Yeah, sorry I was panicking about the thing under the bed. It was nothing—"

"No, I mean at dinner. About learning Japanese."

What? When was the last time I brought that up? Like, six months ago?

"If I'm being frank, I really don't see the point," Dad continues, "but if it really means that much to you, then you should take it in college. I don't know the language well enough to teach you—"

"Wait, where is this coming from?"

"At dinner," Dad says impatiently, like *I'm* the one not making any sense. "You were going on about how you wish I'd bothered to teach you Japanese, so you could show off to your fans on Twitch.

I don't like that that's the reason you're interested in learning—"

"I haven't even eaten dinner, Dad. I *wasn't* at dinner." What the hell is he talking about? Dad isn't one to joke around like this. Is this an early warning sign of dementia? "I haven't asked you about Japanese in months." I would never admit to him that I think it would make me look cool on Twitch.

Dad's eyebrows furrow. "Come on, Vivian. Cut the crap."

I let out an exasperated laugh. "Dad, I literally have no idea what you're talking about."

"Instead of being mad at me for not teaching you Japanese, maybe you should be grateful. You know how hard it was growing up here in the eighties? You kids have it easy these days." He points at my desk. "Be off the computer by nine p.m., and think about how good you have it." Dad turns around and walks away.

I stare as he walks down the hall. WTF is going on? My pulse quickens. Either I'm going insane, everyone else is, or some freaky shit is happening around here. I sit on my bed and FaceTime Bri. After a couple rings, she picks up.

"Sup." She's lying on the couch, *SVU* playing in the background. "You tell Ash to go back to creep land and leave you alone?" She tosses a palmful of popcorn into her mouth.

"I don't think he's the one doing this."

She wipes her mouth, her brows knitting. "Really? Then it has to be your Twitch superfan." She shudders. "Report it. Get a restraining order. Now."

I hesitate. Even if BobbitWorm was hacking my Instagram and stealing my clothes, he couldn't make my dad think I was at dinner when I wasn't, picking fights with him about Japanese. No. Something else is going on, something stranger. "So there's this other weird thing that just happened. . . ."

"What?" Bri stares at me eagerly. "Spit it out."

"My dad swears I was just at dinner. But I wasn't."

Bri gestures for me to continue.

"Did you hear me? My dad saw me at dinner, but I wasn't there."

"So? He's old. He's probably confusing tonight with another night."

"No, he swears I was there and said I was talking about things I most definitely was not."

"Okay?" Bri says, the interest in her voice waning. Her eyes flick to the TV. "So maybe you grabbed some food before you went to interrogate Ash, and you're the one who forgot."

I groan. She's not getting it.

Bri looks at me with pity. "Girl, get some rest. This tired hot mess look is not it."

I glance at myself in the camera. She's right. My eyes are bloodshot, my hair frazzled.

"And seriously, file a police report. I'll go with you tomorrow, okay?" Bri's mom yells for her in the background. "Got to go. Love you." Bri blows me a kiss.

I massage my face. I don't blame Bri. I'm not exactly making the most sense and she's always been the pragmatic one. My eyes lock on that stupid *MST3K* sweatshirt, trying to make sense of its reappearance and Dad saying I was at dinner. What the hell is happening? With all the weirdness going on, it's almost like I'm being haunted, but that's nuts, right?

There's probably only one person who might be able to make some sense of all this. Who won't think I'm crazy.

I call Ash.

"Malevolent spirits love people with emotional baggage," Ash says, his voice brimming with excitement like he'd been hoping I'd call. "And when I saw that 'scratch' on your arm, and you know, everything you've got going on with your . . ."

"Sister's death," I deadpan. I can talk about the fact that she died, just not the circumstances.

"Yeah. That's the first thing I thought—you've got something evil following you, and with all you've been through recently, you're like a sizzling demon buffet."

"Demon?" The image of that dead guy with the orange eyes under my bed flashes in my mind. I move from the bed to the computer chair. It's absolutely bonkers to think there's a demon lurking around, but what other explanation is there? That BobbitWorm is logging in to my Instagram account with no trace, creeping through my window to take my clothes, and got my dad to play along with some "oh I just saw you at dinner" prank? Nope. Don't think so. I hate to admit it, but Ash's explanation is the one that makes sense.

"And if it is a demon, then what do I do about it?" I lock my bedroom door and turn on the lights, which makes me feel 1 percent safer.

"That . . . I don't have an answer for."

Great. If the goth, I-love-Satan guy doesn't have answers, then what? "Well, do you, like, know a guy?"

"You think I just have demonologist connections?"

"Well, *yeah.*"

He chuckles. For some annoying reason, his throaty laugh makes me blush.

"Actually, my cousin in Chicago might be able to help us out. Let me text her."

"That'd be awesome." I can hear him typing in the background. "Ash—"

"Uh-huh?"

"Thank you."

"I'm happy to help in these troubling times."

"Look, I really shouldn't have been such an asshole before—" a few rapid buzzes from my phone interrupt me. I swipe my messages open.

Brianna: WTF IS WRONG WITH YOU

Brianna: OMG HOW COULD YOU DO THIS

My heart begins pounding. It must be serious—Bri's breaking out the all-caps.

Me: what are you talking about?? Are you okay?

Ash starts talking again.

"Ash, I've got to go. I'll call you back." I hang up and dial Bri.

She answers, her voice shaky like she's been crying.

"What's wrong?" I plead. "Are you okay?"

Bri doesn't respond, just sniffles. I literally can't handle not knowing what happened. "Please, tell me what's wrong."

"I can't believe that you would do this."

"Do what?!" I yell, frustrated. "What do you think I did?"

Bri hangs up. A second later my phone receives a text from her. I swipe it open. All the blood drains from my face. It's a conversation between me and Eric—well, someone *pretending* to be me, since I definitely did not send these messages.

Me: hey, there's something i wanna tell you

Eric: wat

Me: Bri doesn't deserve a guy as good as you

Eric: ????

Eric: you're joking right?

Me: Bri says you have a nice 🍆. I wanna see

My phone buzzes again with another screenshot from Bri. Bile gurgles in my throat. It's a selfie sent from "me" to Eric. In the picture, I'm sitting at my computer chair wearing my missing Louise hat and a white tank top, nips poking through, seductively smirking at the camera. I've literally never smiled like that in my life. I study the picture, looking for signs to prove it was photoshopped or AI generated. But there are no blurs, no choppy edges, no extra fingers. My hands go numb from anxiety.

This is impossible.

Every detail from the freckle on my cheek to the mole on my collarbone to the tiny roll of my underarm fat—it's all undeniably the same as my body.

I call Bri again. "Please don't hang up. Just listen to me—I did *not* sext Eric. This isn't me. It's whoever's pranking and stalking me, I SWEAR."

"Oh really? Then why are the pictures from your Twitch DMs? Seriously, no one even uses Twitch whispers other than you."

"I don't know," I stammer. "It's a hacker; someone made this picture! It's not me!" The phrase *it's a demon!* crosses my mind, but I don't say it out loud. It still sounds too crazy.

"You know what? My first thought was that it's photoshopped too. It's what I wanted to believe." Bri's voice cracks. "But then I thought about how you were staring at Eric at Mason's party

You're jealous of us, aren't you?"

I flinch. "Bri, I—"

"What is wrong with you? I thought we were best friends."

"We *are* best friends—"

She scoffs. "Is this a new thing, or have you always been a slut?"

I gasp. Did Bri really just call me the S-word? I thought we were both abolitionists of that label. I stammer for a response, but before I can speak, she hangs up on me.

I look at the picture again, stomach churning. Every detail from my freckles to my greenish-gray hair—it's exactly me. Except the eyes. They're too dark, the irises too big, consuming the whites of my eyes. I shudder. In the bathroom, I splash cold water on my face, Bri's words echoing through my mind. *How could you do this to me?* I'm almost mad at her for believing I would sext Eric. She's smart enough to know I'd never do that—but that's also the problem: Bri is logical. She's going to need hard evidence to believe me.

I pat my face on a towel, then freeze. There's a sound to my right: a faint, raspy breathing. I turn toward the shower. Someone's standing behind the curtain, their silhouette visible through the sheer, light blue fabric.

"Mom?" I say. "Is that you?" My parents have their own bathroom, but maybe one of them needed to use mine for some reason. "Dad, are you in there?"

No response, just a ragged breathing that quickens.

"Hello?" I take a step back.

The curtain rustles. The shape of a hand forms in the fabric, pushing forward, reaching for me. I grip the edge of the curtain and whip it open, yelling, "Who the fuck are you?!"

Nothing's there. I look to the drain and up to the ceiling. What the hell was making that shadow then, and that breathing? I did not just imagine that. I turn back to the bathroom counter to see myself staring back at me in the mirror, grinning.

I'm not smiling.

Goosebumps erupt over my skin. I cover my mouth. The reflection doesn't. Nope, no, uh-uh.

I scream and run down the stairs and out the front door.

"Whoa," Ash says, his face turning red as I show him the picture Bri has of "me." I forgot that my nips are shooting through my tank top in the pic and quickly put my phone back in my pocket.

"Something really messed up is going on—first of all, that picture is not me. I mean, it is. But I did not take that picture. And I sure as hell did not send it to Bri's boyfriend." My heart aches from Bri believing I would really do that, but the evidence is so stacked against me, I can't really blame her. There's only one thing I can do—clear my name, and I need Ash's help.

Ash steps out of his apartment, quietly shutting the door behind him.

"I'm sorry I came over again. You must think I'm insane—maybe I am!" I throw my hands up. "I'm seeing dead guys under my bed, weird shit in the mirror, and now that Bri's turned against me and there's someone out there ruining my life, I don't know who else to ask for help—"

"Whoa back up—dead guys under your bed?" Ash says, strangely excited.

"Well, one dead guy, and yeah, I think that's what I saw. Unless it was my imagination."

"Step one when dealing with the supernatural: Nothing is 'just your imagination.' That's what the malevolent entity wants you to think. Let me guess, it disappeared once you double-checked to see if it was there?"

I nod, my muscles tensing. I really wanted to believe that didn't happen.

"Trust what you see." Ash taps his glasses. "And I got a hold of my cousin. She works at an occult shop in Chicago, gives psychic consultations and stuff. I was going to have you call her, but she said she has to see the wound in person—"

"We could ditch school tomorrow."

"Uhhh, I was thinking more like Thursday night? If I get any more truancies, my mom said she'll sell my car. She's working an overnight flight to Florida on Thursday, so we can leave right after school. Can you tell your parents you're at a friend's place or something?"

"Yeah. You're sure you want to come with me? Because I could just go see your cousin myself—"

"I'm coming. Haven't seen Addison in a while. My mom thinks she's a 'bad influence.' Besides . . ." Ash takes my hand and pushes the sleeve up to reveal my scabs. His touch sends a warm jolt down my spine.

"It sounds weird, but I've always wanted to take on a demon." Ash studies the scabs with a look of admiration. "I always thought I was ripe to attract one, but hey"—he smiles—"I'll take what I can get as sidekick."

Bri doesn't sit with me at lunch, and because we've been best friends since middle school and have had literally every single lunch together, I don't have a backup lunch buddy. Loneliness tightens around me as I observe the cafeteria bustling with chatter and friends grouped together. Three bites into my sandwich, Eric and Bri walk by, holding hands. He probably proved to her that he didn't reciprocate "my" advances and so only I had to experience Bri's wrath. Maybe if I try explaining the hacker/demon situation in person, I can get through to her.

Eric gets up for the soda machine, leaving Bri alone at a table, picking at her salad and scrolling on her phone. I make my move.

"Hey." I approach the table, holding on to my backpack straps for support. "I know I already said this on the phone, but please, you have to believe me. I would never send messages like that to Eric."

Bri's eyes don't move from her phone. If it weren't for the flicker of her jaw muscle, I wouldn't think she even heard me.

"Please, just talk to me." My voice starts to crack.

Bri shifts to look behind her, completely ignoring me. "Hey, babe!" she calls to Eric. "Can you get me a Coke Zero?" Bri turns back to her phone like I'm not here at all.

My chest aches like she just chucked a brick at my sternum. I turn and speed walk to the library, tears forming in my eyes. I find an empty table behind the history bookshelves and open my laptop. In times of crisis, when a demon's ruining my life and my best friend thinks I sexted her boyfriend and hates my guts—I need Twitch now more than ever.

I scroll through all the livestreamers, looking for familiar names. What ever happened to my nemesis, GinnySnow? My insides churn, remembering how everything that went wrong the day Riley died was all because of my rivalry with her. Maybe GinnySnow gave up streaming to pursue a *real job* or something. Before I can dwell on that more, KirbyXXX goes live in *Call of Duty*. Bleh.

KirbyXXX used to be one of my favorite story-rich gamers, but then she went all mainstream, and now all she does is play bland overrated games while bouncing around in a bikini top. It's all about the streaming, not the gaming. Even though I want—even need—streamer stardom, I'm not going to sink that low.

"Every time I die," KirbyXXX smirks at the camera, "I'm going to do ten jumping jacks." She's wearing a neon green bikini and looks amazing, her blond hair blown out, brows and lashes freshly done. Of course, the chat is popping.

Can't wait

Oh yes please

Subscribing now!!!!

When are you getting more merchandise?

"Aww guys. I should have a new line of plushies soon and just you wait—" She winces. "Oh nooo." The screen flashes red as her operator gets knifed in the back. "Welp. You know what that means."

I click out of the window, jealous of how many viewers she has. I don't have the sort of confidence it takes to jump around in a bikini on camera, but that type of viewer engagement brings subscribers in droves. If I'm ever going to help Mom and Dad out of debt, I need to start thinking outside the box. I turn to a fresh page in my notebook and write STREAMING ENTERTAINMENT IDEAS and a series of bullet points:

PUSH-UPS EVERY DEATH? (ON KNEES)

SQUATS? (RIP LEGS)

Or maybe I need to think beyond exercise and do something zany like a flash round of Pictionary. I circle that last idea.

Before Riley's death, I had enough subscribers to buy myself Panera Bread regularly, which is no small feat. Now, I'm basically starting over, other than the handful of OG subscribers (my cousins and BobbitWorm) who stuck around for my offline period. But the kind of money I need to make requires way more subscribers, like *way* more than before. I practically beam imagining the look on Mom and Dad's faces when I tell them I've paid off their mortgage. Dad will have to admit that he was wrong about my "little streaming hobby" being a "waste of time." And it'll be my way of atoning for killing Riley, but they'll never have to know that part.

I take a selfie and post it to my Instagram story with the caption: New Stream Tonight!!! Tune in!!!! The gamers who earn a lucrative living on Twitch stream at least forty hours a week, so I have to start fitting in as many hours as I can after school.

The bell rings. I shut my laptop and put it back in my bag, excited for this day to end so I can get home and try this Pictionary streaming idea. I walk down the hall toward chemistry class. A series of rapid dings chime from my phone. I pull it out to put it back on Do Not Disturb. I gasp. My screen is full of notifications.

My heart skips. Am I going viral?

I open TikTok. I have dozens of DMs and comments on a new video. I read one of the messages: what the hell is wrong with you?

What? Maybe my latest stream offended someone. Oh god—what if I'm getting canceled? A blaring alarm reverberates through the hall. The loud sound makes me jolt and drop my phone. Shit. I bend down to pick it up. An automated female voice speaks through the intercom, repeating the line:

Please exit the building as quickly as possible. This is not a drill.

"Is there a fire?!" A girl yells behind me.

A boy whoops. "Hell yeah, let's just go home now."

A teacher holds open the door, gesturing frantically for students to exit. A panicked line forms for the door. I join the crowd. Where is the fire? What the hell is going on?

Feedback from the intercom screeches through the speakers overhead. A serious male voice speaks over the alarm.

Vivian Reynolds. Please report to the principal's office. Immediately.

I fidget with my backpack straps as I rush up the stairs to the principal's office, avoiding eye contact with all the other students fleeing the building. Why are they calling me to the office if there's a fire? My skin crawls with anxiety. Am I in trouble? Surely, this is a mistake, right? I've never been in trouble for anything. But what if it's something worse? What if something happened to Mom or Dad? Dread knots in my stomach and I speed up, bursting through the principal's office.

Dad is here, pacing the room, his face pale and grave.

Oh my god. What if Mom is hurt? Or dead?

"Sit," the principal orders from behind the desk, his voice stern, definitely not the compassionate tone of one about to inform a student their mother has died, which soothes some of my anxiety but starts a whole new spiral.

"What's going on?" I say, still standing. "Dad, why are you here?"

Dad starts to speak but the principal cuts him off, and that's when I notice the police officer standing in the back of the room.

"Place your backpack on the table," the principal says.

"Why?"

"Do it. *Now.*" The police officer grips the gun at his hip.

I quickly unloop my straps and set the backpack on the table, my hands shaking.

"Even though this might be all talk, young lady, we take every threat to student safety very seriously." The police officer cautiously approaches my backpack.

"I literally have no idea what's going on." I look to Dad for reassurance, but he's massaging his face, glasses pushed up onto his head.

The principal scoffs. "Well, you should, considering you're the one who posted your intentions."

"What?" I whip out my phone and open TikTok again. My stomach drops when I see the video that has three likes and thousands of views. It's a screen record of a text conversation between me and Bri.

Brianna: did you see that Tristan is dating Amy Chen now? i swear he's got that yellow fever

Me: lol. he's gotta know if that TAP is real or not

Brianna: seriously. so gross

Me: maybe we'll luck out and he'll get hit by a bus

Brianna: lol

I remember the conversation from around five months ago, but all the time stamps say they're from this morning. What I don't remember is this next part:

Me: but we can't rely on luck

Me: if i want him to die, i have to make it happen

Me: i know how to make a pipe bomb

Me: steel water pipe, fill it with nails

Me: gunpowder

Me: i'll make it today

Me: put it in the boys' locker room. take him out and all his gross baseball friends too

"What the hell?" I drop my phone on the desk. "I was hacked—I never said any of that!"

"My daughter was joking," Dad says to the cop. "She's into some dark content online. We shouldn't let her play so many violent games—"

"No, Dad, I was literally hacked!"

Dad frowns at me. "And who would do that, Vivian? Why?"

I stammer for an answer. If this had happened last week, I would've been sure it was GinnySnow, trying to have me swatted to get back at me for copying her blindfold stream. But considering all the weirdness going on, it has to be the same person—the same *thing*—that sent the fake texts to Bri.

"Tristan, he was your boyfriend?" the police officer asks.

My stomach tightens. "Umm, sort of." I look away from Dad. He's firm about meeting and assessing every boy who's even remotely in my friend zone, and I never told him about Tristan at all.

"And who is 'Brianna'?" the police officer barks.

"Brianna Davis," the principal answers. "Another senior."

"And what is 'TAP'?" the officer asks.

My face reddens.

"Answer him!" Dad says.

"I don't know, just some dumb thing me and Bri made up." *Please, god, just leave it at that.*

The officer's eyes narrow at me. "We'll need to talk to Brianna too." He writes Bri's full name down on his notepad.

Oh fuck. At least Bri will be able to corroborate my story that I never sent these messages, but the chances of her ever forgiving me are literally disintegrating. What if this somehow ends up on her record and interferes with her chance of getting into college? Guilt gnaws my insides. "Bri has nothing to do with this, I swear."

"We'll be the judge of that." The officer snaps latex gloves onto his hands. He opens my backpack, feeling inside all the pockets. "It's clear," he says to the principal. "But keep the students evacuated until we've searched all locker rooms and classrooms." He pulls out my laptop. "What is your PIN?"

"1111."

He unlocks the laptop and opens my search history, which is a relief because he's not going to find anything incriminating. Just search results for top Twitch streamers, horror games, and images of Light Yagami shirtless—which isn't what it seems like.

My search history loads, and my stomach falls to my butt.

How to make a pipe bomb

What batteries to use for pipe bombs

Will one pipe bomb kill five teenage boys

My head swirls with nausea. "That wasn't me!" I say, realizing too late that those words are what a guilty person would say. "I mean someone's been hacking my stuff! They planted it there! Someone's trying to swat me to ruin my reputation." I'm trying to stay composed, but my throat tightens, cutting off my air, making me sound squeaky and desperate. "Please, you have to believe me."

"Sir." The officer ignores me and looks to Dad. "We'll need to send a bomb squad to search your house."

I'm grounded for life.

The bomb squad searched the house and didn't find anything. Thank god. I half expected there to be an actual bomb in my bedroom with my signature on it, but there was nothing, which in some way might be even more unsettling—what terrible thing is coming next?

I stand on a chair by the air vent in my room, waiting to overhear Mom and Dad talk about me. Am I suspended? Expelled? Going to jail? I literally have no idea. I've been banished to my room and told nothing. No one believes that I was hacked because none of my devices show any trace of being logged in to anywhere other than my phone and room.

"What did the police say about criminal charges?" Mom asks Dad. Their voices carry surprisingly well from the vent. I haven't eavesdropped on them in months. The last time I did, I heard a conversation I've been trying to forget ever since. It was a couple days after Riley died.

"It's my fault," Mom said, her voice cracking. "If I hadn't lost that button—"

"Stop it," Dad said, his tone sharp.

I didn't want to keep listening, but I had to know if they still believed my lie.

"It was my carelessness—"

"Fine!" Dad yelled. "It was your fault. Are you happy?"

Mom sobbed.

"Either way, it doesn't change anything." Dad sounded so tired.

Silence.

I curled into a ball on the floor, sobbing, wanting to die. My lie had worked—it shouldn't have, but it did, and now my parents were carrying my burden. If the truth ever got out, if they knew I'd made them blame themselves for what I had done, they would never forgive me. They'd hate me.

Now, I stand on my tippy-toes, craning my ear closer to the vent. They probably hate me anyway because they think I plotted to bomb the boy's locker room.

"The police said this was a false alarm," Dad says. "She's suspended from school for the rest of the week, but there are no legal ramifications. I was going to let Viv know tonight."

"No," Mom says. "Let her sweat."

Wow, really Mom? I guess I can see how from her point of view, I deserve that.

"Only for another day or so. This is our fault," Mom continues. "We never should have let her think she could stream video games for a career, all that shooting and killing." Mom's voice cracks. "How did we let it get to this point?"

I cover my mouth. These last few hours, I've been wallowing over how the whole school thinks I'm the Unabomber now. I hadn't even thought about how this would affect my parents. Dad has his own business. It basically thrives on word-of-mouth referrals. Will people get their air conditioners installed by the father of the town terrorist? Probably not, because we care so much about nice appearances in the Midwest. No one likes Ash's mom anymore, and I'm pretty sure that's why she makes the forty-five-minute commute to the Ames airport for work, so no one will recognize her. This whole thing might've just ruined Dad's business. *Fuck.*

"How did we not know about this boyfriend?" Dad asks. "Tristan?"

Mom is silent. She knew about Tristan, and we agreed together to put off telling Dad until the time seemed right, which didn't happen since I broke up with Tristan anyway.

"You knew?"

"It wasn't serious," Mom says passively.

"Apparently it was serious if she wants to kill the boy."

I flinch.

"Are you thinking of giving those back to her?" Dad continues. "We need to put our foot down."

I bite my nails. He must be talking about my phone and laptop.

"And I think we should take the desktop too," Dad adds. "No more games. No social life."

My stomach falls. Oh my god, Dad. No. *Please, stand up for me, just once, Mom.* But my hopes aren't high. Last year, Mom was going to take me to TwitchCon. But then Dad read about how some of the biggest names there were also OnlyFans stars and he said there was no way Mom could take me to Vegas to idolize "porn stars." I begged and pleaded with them, but Mom sided with Dad.

"I don't know," Mom says. "She needs the games. Her friends. Brianna." My heart swells. Mom's actually coming through for me.

"I worry that if we take too much from her . . ." Mom pauses, and when she speaks again, her voice shakes. "We might lose this daughter too."

My heart aches. I'd never turn my back on Mom and Dad like that, not even if they grounded me.

"Could you imagine . . ." Mom continues, her voice heavy, "if Viv did something drastic? Tried to hurt herself because we came down too hard?"

I gasp. Mom thinks I might . . . kill myself? The thought fleetingly crossed my mind when I saw the meme Eric Snapchatted of the Unabomber glasses and hoodie photoshopped onto my picture, but I couldn't do that to Mom and Dad. I'm all they have left.

"I hate that you said that," Dad says. "But you might be right. We need to be compassionate. . . . There will be rules, though."

"Yes," Mom agrees.

"No gaming on school nights. No more than two hours of consecutive screen time. And we're confiscating Vivian's phone every night."

Okay, that sucks. I inhale. But I can live with it. And now I know that there are two things I must do. I jump down from the chair and go to my computer.

One, I need my streaming career to flourish more than ever. Dad's going to need my help if his business suffers from this disaster.

Two, whoever—whatever—is ruining my life, I need to stop them. Now.

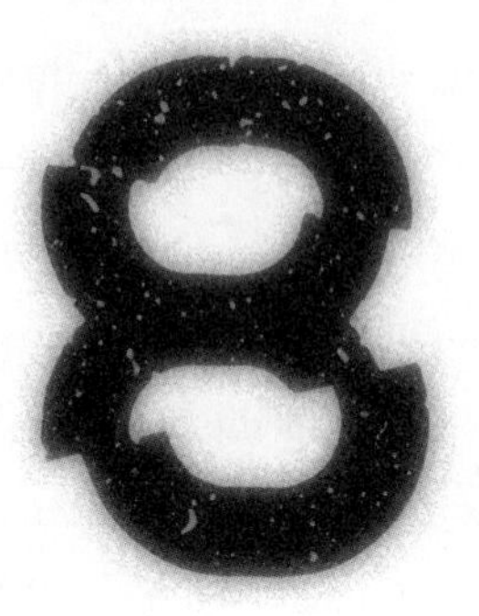

On Thursday night at 9:00 p.m., I creep down stairs silently in my socks. Mom and Dad are lightweights who pass out around 8:30 p.m., and since I'm grounded, telling them that I was going to Bri's wasn't an option, so blatantly sneaking out is my only choice. I carefully open the front door, making sure it doesn't squeak, and step into the night.

It's a three-hour drive to Chicago, and I can't risk breaking down in Ash's POWERED BY SATAN rust bucket and getting stranded, so we're taking my car. I just pray that Mom doesn't wake up and look out the window to see my car missing from the driveway, but I doubt she will. She's been taking a sleeping pill every night since Riley's death. And Dad sleeps like he's been cursed with a torpor spell.

I quietly slip into my car and buckle in, then reach for my phone to connect it to Bluetooth and remember that I don't have it. Dad took it away at 7:00 p.m., like somehow that's going to protect me. Whatever he needs to feel some control, I guess. I slowly pull out of my spot and turn toward Ash's apartment.

The streetlight on the corner flickers out when I get to the stop sign. I roll forward. Another streetlamp fades to black too. *Cheap-ass infrastructure. What do we pay taxes for?* Still, it's unsettling, and I turn on the radio. An Olivia Rodrigo song plays, and I hum along, tapping my fingers to the beat. Static crackles through the radio, then Rodrigo's voice distorts, becoming deep and slow. The radio clicks off. I fidget with the knobs, trying to turn it back on. *Come on, come on.* The radio won't respond. *Why are my hands trembling? It's nothing, just a cheap radio. Definitely not a demon screwing with me.*

Just a couple more miles to Ash's place. I grip the steering wheel with both hands, taking a left turn. Beady orange eyes stare back at me from the gutter. I scream, swerving the car to the right, crashing into a recycling bin. *Shit, shit, shit.* My shaking hand thrusts the car into reverse, and I peel out, leaving a bunch of milk jugs and cardboard scattered on the sidewalk behind me. I should go back and clean that up, but there's a demon after me. I have to get out of here.

I speed several yards away then slow down. Where did it go? I look in the rearview mirror, searching for those orange eyes. *There.* Small glowing eyes blink back at me from the curb. I stop the car, ready to floor it. *What do you want, you evil bastard?* The eyes move closer and out of the shadows. The body is way smaller than it should be for a demon. And it has a tail. And fur. A raccoon. It's a goddamn raccoon.

I can't help but laugh. *Jeez, Viv, ease up*—my breathing stops. A cold hand grips my neck, clamping down on my throat. My eyes bulge, panic shooting through me. I take in a small breath and am hit with the pungent scent of charred, rotten meat. I look in the mirror. The demon's behind me, leaning toward my seat, its long, skinny hand wrapped around my neck. Its mouth is lipless, the skin burned off, its brown pointed teeth in multiple rows like a shark's, wet with bloody saliva. I try to break free, but the demon's grip only tightens. *What the fuck does it want? Why is it doing this to me?*

A truck turns down the street. I try to wave, try to scream for help. Headlights shine through my windshield. The hand releases. I rub my neck, gasping in air. The white Chevy slows to a stop next to my car.

"You okay?" a woman asks, rolling down her window.

"Yeah." I try to sound like nothing just happened, but my body and voice are shaking uncontrollably. "Did you, um, see someone in the seat behind me?" I gesture toward my back seat.

"Like just a moment ago?"

The woman's brows furrow. "No. Just saw you waving like you were in trouble."

"Oh. Right. Well, I'm fine, thanks for checking!" I roll up my window and drive forward, heart pounding. Oh god. Does this mean no one else can see it? Or did I imagine the whole thing because I'm losing my mind?

At the red light, I glance to my side. My passenger seat is ripped, the fabric torn in four lines. Claw marks. I smile. My demon is real. I'm not supposed to be happy about that, but it feels good to have proof and know that I'm not insane.

Ash stands outside on the curb, hoodie pulled up over his head, hands in his pockets.

I frantically wave for him to get inside. I am not sitting alone in this car a second longer.

He opens the passenger-side door, eyeing the seat's shredded fabric before getting in. I drive down the street.

"Something happen to your car?"

"It was in here," I whisper, paranoid that the demon's somehow listening to me. "When I was on my way to get you."

"No way!" Ash says, annoyingly enthused. "Damn, I missed it?"

"It's not cool, Ash! It could've freaking killed me."

"Nah. If it wanted you dead, you would be already."

"Thanks. That makes me feel *much* better."

"Sorry," he mumbles.

A long moment of silence. The blinker ticks as I wait to turn left onto the freeway.

"And I've been wanting to say . . ." Ash starts. "It's really messed up what happened with the whole Tristan thing. This demon really hates you."

"You think?" I say sarcastically, but I am relieved. The night it all went down, I typed the whole disastrous thing out to Ash in a long-winded email. His response: "damn." It's good to know he actually does care.

"What are people saying at school?" I gnaw my lip. I've seen enough Snapchats to know it's not good.

"Well, people think you're a murderous psycho." He chuckles. "It's actually kind of nice to hear them talking shit about someone else other than me."

My face reddens. He doesn't know that I was one of those shit-talkers, but I won't be anymore. Not after all this.

"Tristan's using the whole thing to garner sympathy," Ash continues. "Acting like he needs a flock of bodyguards."

I roll my eyes. Of course.

"But don't worry too much, okay? Addie should be able to help."

"I hope so. On the bright side . . . the whole thing did bring in a few new subscribers to my channel." I also lost a bunch, but I can't even think about that right now. I'm not sure the murder-endorsers are the demographic I want, but I'm taking every little positive I can get right now.

"You're seriously still thinking about your subscriber count with all you have going on?"

"I mean, *yeah*, I still have to think about my future." I keep my eyes on the road but can tell Ash is throwing me a judgmental look. "Streaming is basically my job."

Ash scoffs. "It's not a real job."

I roll my eyes. "You sound like my mom. She's always like 'why don't you get a real job and stream on the side; what are you going to do for health insurance after you're twenty-five, blah blah blah.'"

"At least she cares. My mom doesn't give a shit about my future," Ash says, his tone unusually heavy.

My grip tightens on the steering wheel. It hadn't even occurred to me that Ash and his mom might not have a good relationship after what happened with his dad. I assumed the whole tragedy would've brought them closer together, but it's not like that's what happened with me and my parents. I chew on my lip, searching for something to say, but Ash starts talking again.

"What's so good about streaming anyway? Looks like a pain in the ass."

I tell him the same thing I've told Mom: "I love gaming and I want a career doing something I enjoy. Like, I don't want to be just a warm body at a laptop answering calls and emails. No offense to my mom, but she is not thriving filing people's insurance claims all day."

Ash snorts. "Welcome to life in the capitalist machine. We all have to get by somehow."

"Yeah, and I'm getting by with gaming. What do you want to do for work?"

"I already have a job."

"Oh?" I'd assumed Ash just slept all day and wrote goth guitar ballads. "Where at?"

"The movie theater on Quincy Street. Sucks ass."

"I bet." I've never been to that movie theater. I've heard the AC's always broken and there's a perpetual funk in the air since that's where couples go when their parents are home. "Well, what career do you want? Like, dream job?"

He thinks for a moment. "Guitarist in a metal band, but second to that, something that lets me travel a lot. I want to get out of the Midwest. Maybe I'll be a train conductor."

"Uh-huh." He wants to be a guitarist, but I'm the one with the stupid career goal? The conversation peters out to silence again. "You want to put on some music or something?"

Ash connects his phone to my Bluetooth and turns up Black Sabbath. We agree that we each get thirty minutes of Spotify control. On his turns, it's Shinedown, Atreyu, or Tool. On mine, we listen to Taylor Swift and Dua Lipa, which Ash comments isn't *real* music, but I catch him nodding along to the beat a couple times.

An hour outside of Chicago, we stop at a gas station, so Ash can smoke and I can pee. I buy another Red Bull, thankful that I thought ahead and brought cash so Mom can't track my debit card usage. When I get back to the car, Ash is still in the gas station. I reach for my phone to check Twitch and remember it's back home. Ugh. I massage my empty pocket like I can manifest my phone if I just wish hard enough.

Ash's phone is in the cup holder, unlocked from when he last changed the song. I grab it, open the browser, and go to Twitch. He won't mind; it's not like I'm snooping through his search history. I just need to see if my subscriber count has changed at all, if I'm still listed under "Recommended in Horror."

My thumb hovers over the Search button. I freeze, my pulse pounding in my neck.

No f-ing way.

Under the *What's Hot* live channels—there I am, streaming *LOCKED IN*. But it's not me. It's someone who looks exactly like me. She's in my room, sitting at my gaming chair and wearing my purple bikini top, her makeup done, and somehow the greenish-gray hair even looks decent, down and straightened. WTF. My eyes widen when I see the viewer count: 1,127. I haven't had views like that since last year!

"That's not me!" I scream at the phone, frantically opening

the stream. I try to type in the chat that it's not me, but Ash doesn't have an account so I can't write anything. I can't do anything but watch.

In *LOCKED IN*, the fake me walks her avatar up the staircase of the abandoned apartment building. "It's so spooky. I'm glad you guys are here," she says. I cover my mouth. Her voice even sounds exactly like mine.

wow Viv I love the new look

this isn't Viv's style I don't like it

did you really try to kill ur ex

u can tell viv's japanese she's got dem anime tiddies

put some clothes on where are your parents

shut up prude let girls be free

The subscriber number ticks up, and I feel a reflexive jolt of excitement. But I know I shouldn't. This is bad. This evil bitch is ruining—now *stealing*—my life.

I turn to see Ash heading back toward the car. I roll the window down. "Ash, LOOK!"

He speeds up. "What are you doing on my phone—"

I gesture at the livestream.

"Oh shit." He drops his bag of Doritos and grabs the phone from me.

"Download Twitch, quick! I need to log in and tell everyone it's not really me!" Maybe I can go live and prove that I'm really somewhere else.

"Damn. The stream ended." He shows me the phone, and the livestream has gone to a black screen.

I groan, slumping in my seat.

"But I took a screenshot." He shows me the phone again and there's a picture of me at my computer desk, leaning forward, smirking and staring straight into the camera. It's the eyes that give her away. They're a shade too dark.

A little before midnight, we cross into the city and get stuck at the longest red light. My knee shakes with impatience as I watch the clock on the dashboard slowly ticking up.

"How's my subscriber count doing?" I can't believe that one stream brought in over a thousand viewers. What if my fans like the demon more than me? My stomach knots. What if I'm boring and bland and the evil fake version of me is better? The thought makes me want to cry.

"You got three more. Seriously, how can you care about that right now?"

"I know, I know." I can't exactly explain to him that I need subscribers to atone for killing my sister, that it's the only thing that lets me live with myself. "It's complicated. Do you think it's weird that more people were watching that stream than my regular ones?"

"It's just cuz her tits were out. Sex sells."

I groan. Ugh, he's right. Maybe I should suck it up and doll myself up more.

"But people would've gotten bored and soon they would've moved on to one of the other thousands of basic channels. Your streams are way more interesting. You can tell you care about the game and the small details. You, like, *know* horror, the ambience and stuff. That's what matters."

"Wait, you've watched my streams?" I turn to look at him.

He purses his lips. "I might've come across them once or twice."

I smile. Still, the viewer count thing is really getting to me. "But why stream as me? What the hell does that accomplish?" All it did was make me insecure AF. Maybe that was the point.

"Getting in your head. It's all psychological games with these demons until . . ."

"Until what?"

"Until they're done playing with their prey."

My knuckles whiten around the steering wheel.

"It's gonna be okay." Ash points to the parking lot of a small strip mall. "Pull in there."

There's a cannabis shop, a thrift store, a karate place, and to the very far left in purple neon: ONE STOP OCCULT SHOP. A few candles and plastic skulls line the inside of the windowsill. A poster in the window reads OUIJA MIDNIGHT MADNESS. It looks cheesy as hell, more like a Halloween store than the place that's going to save me, but it's the only lead we have.

I park the car. "Alright. Let's do this."

The door chimes when we walk through. The lighting is dim. Dusty bookshelves line the walls. The scent of sweet, woody incense hangs thick in the air. Several goths sit in a circle on the floor, a Ouija board between them. A black cat sleeps curled on a table, decks of tarot cards beside its tail.

Ash approaches the register, where a young woman with purple space buns leans against the counter, scrolling on her phone. Her pierced eyebrows raise.

"We're here to see Addison. I'm Ash."

"Back there." The woman pops her gum and points toward a hallway behind a beaded curtain. The sign above the door reads PSYCHIC CONSULTATIONS.

"Umm, how much is this going to cost?" I ask Ash. I brought enough cash for caffeine and gas, not much else.

"She said it's on the house."

"Sweet. Thanks."

We pass through the curtain and enter a small, dark room that smells like weed. A woman in her mid-twenties sits at a round table, playing a game on her phone. "Hey, Ash!" She stands and wraps him in a hug. "You've gotten so big!"

She reaches her hand out to shake mine, her wrists covered in several silver bracelets. "I'm Addison. You must be Vivian." A red headband holds her dark hair out of her face. She's strikingly pretty with the same sharp angular eyebrows as Ash.

"Yeah. Nice to meet you."

"She's cute." Addison winks at Ash, taking a seat at the table.

He gives a short grunt in response and sits in the chair across from Addison. I pull the other wooden chair near the wall to join them.

"How's Linda?" Addison asks Ash. "Still a flight attendant?"

"Yeah, and she's doing fine, I guess. On her usual bullshit. She's selling essential oils now, too, but pretty sure buying the product costs way more than she makes."

Addison frowns. "She knows you came to see me?"

Ash shakes his head.

"Probably for the best. Maybe I'll come down for Christmas. Anywho . . ." Her eyes trail to me. "Ash gave me some details, but please, start from the beginning. Tell me what ails you." Addison rests her chin on her fist.

"Well . . ." I start, pausing to figure out how to put all the weirdness of these last few days into words. "At first, I thought I had a stalker, since someone sent messages from my account posing as me, and then I felt like someone was watching me."

I go into how the sexts were sent to Bri's boyfriend, how someone who looks exactly like me was livestreaming on my channel, how there was a scary dead guy with too many teeth under my bed and in my car, and how the whole school thinks I plotted to kill my ex.

Addison nods with sympathy, eyes widening at certain details.

"Show her the mark." Ash gestures at my arm.

I roll up my sleeve. "And then there's this. I got it during sleep paralysis. The night before things started getting weird."

Addison gasps and takes my forearm, studying the mark. "Ah. Mise en abyme. See this spiral pattern. How it trails inward?"

I hadn't noticed that, mostly since it's ugly as shit, and I'd rather not look at the wound, but I turn my head to see it from her perspective and . . . yeah, I don't see whatever she's talking about.

"I took a screenshot from when the demon was livestreaming as Vivian." Ash holds up his phone, showing the picture to Addison.

Addison's eyes trail from the picture on his phone to me, from the picture back to me. Then she and Ash lock eyes, her gaze serious. Ash tenses beside me.

"Vivian." Addison sucks in a breath, like the words she's about to say are difficult to get out. "I believe you're being targeted by a demon that takes your form. A doppelgänger."

"A what?" I've heard the word before in Edgar Allan Poe stories, but how can this be happening to me IRL?

"It's a mimic." Addison places her hand on mine. "They've been around since the dawn of time. Some are tricksters. Some are vengeful. Some are . . ."—she glances at the picture on Ash's phone again—"evil incarnate."

"Why me?" I ask, not sure if I want to scream or cry. "Why can't evil incarnate torment literally anyone else?"

"Have you bought any wooden chests at a yard sale recently? Any old porcelain dolls?" Addison asks.

"No."

"Have you made any suspicious deals lately? Make any confessions to a mystery entity that approached you in the mall or someplace you feel safe?"

"No."

"Hmm." Addison frowns. "Demons are stealthy with how they infiltrate their victims' lives. So I want you to think hard."

I rack my mind, but there have been no chests, dolls, or mall confessions. Wait. I did make that confession in *LOCKED IN*—but that's a video game. An offline video game. That can't be it, right?

"I guess I did make a 'confession' about something," I air quote and roll my eyes like it wasn't as serious as how I killed my baby sister and covered it up. "In a video game. All I did was type a few paragraphs to an NPC when the game prompted me. That's all I can think of."

Addison stares at me. "What did the NPC ask exactly?"

"That I tell it a secret. A 'dark and true' secret."

"And what did you type in response?" Addison's voice lowers in seriousness.

I shift uncomfortably. "Does it matter? It was just a video game." I laugh, but the game comes back to me in icy-hot stabbing memory flashes: the cloaked NPC, those beady orange eyes beneath its hood, the sleep paralysis I had the same night I first played. *Oh fuck.*

Addison's eyes narrow at me. "Demons are smart, ancient entities. They're always evolving new ways to feed on human misery."

I double over in my chair, the air suddenly hard to breathe. Could it really be that stupid game? I grip my temples. Why did I *actually* tell it my darkest secret?

"Let me get this straight." Ash looks at me. "You told a secret to a demon on your computer, but you won't tell it to us?"

"I thought it was just a game!" I groan. "And no, I'm not telling you my secret." I massage my face. "Now what?"

"Well . . ." Addison chews her thumbnail. "Doppelgängers typically move on from their victims when they've achieved what they want, most likely your insanity or death. So you'll want to kill it before it kills you," she says, like it's as simple as spraying some ants with Raid.

"Um, okay, *can* it be killed?"

"Of course, in a sense."

"How?"

"That, I'm not sure. But it's best to have some physical protection." She stands and walks to a cluttered shelf where she picks up one of many shiny novelty daggers, a serpent etched into the handle. The dagger looks ridiculous, like a prop for a fantasy movie. "A gift for my favorite cousin's friend." She puts the dagger in a reusable grocery bag, handing it to me. It's heavier than I expected.

"And this could kill it?"

"Oh, no." Addison gives me a pitiful look. "But iron burns demons. So it may provide some self-defense." She gives me a reassuring nod. "You said that the doppelgänger first sent seductive texts to this Bri person's boyfriend, right?"

"Yeah, she's my best friend."

Addison nods. "I suspect your doppelgänger will cause havoc with your loved ones in an attempt to leave you isolated." She squeezes my shoulder. "Use that to your advantage. Good luck."

"Okay, thanks. And thank you for your time, and this." I gesture with the bag. Ash stands, starting to walk out with me.

"Ash, a word?" Addison says. "I'll keep him for just a minute, promise." She smiles at me.

I leave the room and browse the bookshelves. If the demon latched on to me through the video game—then what . . . ? Do I play it again? Try to kill it in the game? Kill it in the game and it dies in real life? I laugh at my own ridiculous logic, and that turns into a sob. What the hell am I going to do? I look at the knife in the bag. Am I supposed to engage the doppelgänger in one-on-one combat? Yeah, right. Those points are not in my skill tree. I pace the aisles of bookshelves, running through what Addison said about the doppelgänger targeting my loved ones. Her words might be giving me an idea. . . .

Ash walks out, hands in his pockets, head hanging slightly.

"What's up? What'd she want?"

"She doesn't want me to—eh, never mind. Let's go?"

"Sure." Doesn't feel like my business to pry, and I suspect I know what she said anyway: for Ash to stay out of my doppelgänger problem, which is smart, and I get it if that's what she said, but selfishly, I need Ash's help.

We walk outside and I unlock the car.

"So who do you think the doppelgänger will try to make hate you next?" Ash asks, opening the passenger door and getting in.

My parents come to mind. But the Tristan murder threat made them think I'm an unhinged asshole, so that was enough, right? I can't risk it hurting my parents more—I definitely can't have it going after my mee-maw in Des Moines, which means I need to get ahead of it. Take control of which relationships it's trying to destroy and use that to my advantage, like Addison said.

I sit in the driver's seat and turn to look Ash in the eyes. "Will you be my boyfriend?"

Ash's face turns red.

"Not for real," I add, my own face warming as I realize that the plan in my mind sounds way different out loud. "We'll just make the demon *think* you are."

Ash nods, realizing what I'm asking. "Then we can lure it someplace."

"And we can expose it, prove it wasn't me in the pictures, and . . ." I feel for the handle of the knife in the bag. "Then we kill it."

"Take a picture of us," I say to Ash when I pull up to his apartment. It's 4:02 a.m., and all I want to do is sleep, but I need to get this ball rolling with luring the demon to him.

He swipes his phone to the camera and holds it up in selfie mode. I press my cheek against his, the strands of his hair tickling my face. I'm smiling. He's glaring.

"Smile," I order from the corner of my mouth.

He gives a quick smirk and snaps the pic.

"Email it to me," I say. "So my dad doesn't see the text and get nosy, and I'll post it today."

"Won't your parents wonder how you got a boyfriend while you were grounded?"'

Ugh. Good point. "I'll just tell them we took the picture before I got in trouble." I wave my hand flippantly. Dad isn't on Instagram, thankfully.

Ash shrugs, getting out of my car.

I speed back home, barely braking at the stop signs. I'd rather get a ticket than end up with the demon in the car again. I park in the driveway and quietly go inside the house. Once I'm upstairs, I press my ear to my parents' door. They're snoring softly in there. Perfect. It's like I never left. I tiptoe down the hall to my room, feeling a teeny bit guilty for sneaking around their backs. But desperate times call for desperate lying.

In my room, I inspect my desk chair and gaming area, searching for clues the doppelgänger might have left behind. I can't find anything out of place. Even my purple bikini top is back in the drawer. I shiver. If I hadn't seen that stream, I wouldn't have ever known the doppelgänger had been in my room.

I slide into my desk chair, staring at the *LOCKED IN* icon on my desktop's home screen. If the doppelgänger really is from the game, then should I play it again? Could there be something useful in the game? It's not like things can really get any worse if I try. I double click the icon.

Error: Program not found.

Huh? I open my documents and search for the file, but all traces of it are erased from my computer. *Shit.* The game is gone.

But why? And what does that change? Nothing. I still have to figure out how to defeat the doppelgänger, and that means getting ahead of it with Ash.

I open the email from Ash, downloading the selfie to my computer. In the picture, my eyelids are swollen with a desperate need for sleep. Ash's eyes are red, so he looks like his usual self: stoned or tired. We look haggard really, but I look kind of cute and . . . Ash does too? Now that I'm thinking of him as my pretend boyfriend, emphasis on the *pretend*, I can't help but notice his strong nose and jawline, the warmth of his brown eyes, those enviable eyebrows. Aside from the dark circles under his eyes, Ash is actually kind of, dare I say, attractive?

I apply a bright Instagram filter so we look a little livelier. Now, I just need a cute caption. When Tristan and I used to post pics together, I always wrote some gushy caption about how much fun we were having, how he was such a sweet, caring guy, lies, lies, lies. I want to write something good, but I'm literally two seconds from falling asleep, so I insert a row of hearts and click the Share button. Hopefully, it will be enough to pique the doppelgänger's interest. What will Bri think? Maybe seeing this picture of me and Ash will be enough to make her reach out to me . . . but probably not if she still believes I was trying to bang Eric.

I refresh my Instagram page, checking if anyone's liked the pic yet. Of course not, because it's 4:25 a.m. and the normal humans are asleep, but still, I just need to know if this plan is going to work. I massage my knuckles. How can I make Ash even more enticing to the doppelgänger? It went after my friendship with Bri—we have years of history there: pictures from our trip to Disney World together, *Magic: The Gathering* games archived on my YouTube channel. To really pull this off, I need to make Ash irresistible.

I send an Instagram DM to Ash: hey! thanks for helping out with everything tonight. Addison was great. one more favor to ask—will you be a guest on my Twitch channel?

Ash: why

I start to type "to lure my doppelgänger" but quickly tap the backspace, remembering how the doppelgänger sent messages to Bri from my account. I changed my password, but what if it's still somehow reading all my messages? A chill runs down my back.

Me: for you know what—let's not talk about it on here

I rest my eyes a moment, waiting for him to respond. My desktop chimes.

Ash: fine. you ever stop thinking about your subscriber count?

No. I reply: yeah! but this isn't about that. i want to declare our LOVE publicly.

I want to put "love" in quotes, but he should get what I'm saying.

Ash: ok. passing out now. but i'm down for tonight

Me: kk :)

I kick my shoes off and crawl into bed. Getting suspended

sort of worked in my favor—there's no way I could get up for school in two hours.

When I wake, it's unusually cold in the room. I glance at my iPad, squinting from the sudden brightness. 1:03 p.m. My black curtains keep most of the sunlight out. I walk to my desk, yawning the grogginess away, and sit in front of my computer.

My reflection stares back at me on the dark screen, my hair sticking up in all different directions. I jiggle the mouse, but the monitor doesn't respond. *Ugh.* A two-thousand-dollar computer should not be this laggy. I tap the spacebar a few times.

In my reflection on the screen, a hand reaches up from behind me, smoothing the flyaway hairs. A cold touch grazes my head. I spin around, my heart racing. No one's there. I touch my hair reflexively, turning back to the computer.

A faint, raspy feminine voice comes from the desktop speaker.

Come closer.

In here.

What the hell? This must be an ad, a video playing on a tab I didn't close. I lean closer to the screen.

Hi, the voice says. *Where'd you go last night?*

The hairs on my arms stand up. I hit Enter several times, trying again to wake up the damn monitor. Come on, turn on, turn on, turn on. Static crackles across the screen, black and blue pixels.

Did you like my stream?

"Shut up!" I mutter, mashing the Volume Down button.

That's not very nice.

A cold hand wraps through my hair, sharp nails pressing into my scalp. I try to turn my head, but the grip is strong, holding me in place. My throat tightens, my heart hammering.

The screen turns from static to black. In the reflection, a figure stands behind me, its shoulders narrow, the same frame as mine. My hands tremble as I try to push myself back off the desk. "Get off me—"

The grip on my head tightens, yanks my hair backward, then slams my face forward. My nose smashes into the desk with a wet crunch. My vision turns white.

"Fuck!" I shout, standing and blinking the pain away. Warm wetness drips from my nose down my chin.

"Get away from me!" I rush to the window, whipping open the curtain and letting in the sunlight, as if that might help. I remind myself it's a demon, not a vampire. Blurry-eyed, I grab the umbrella leaning against the wall, holding it up like a weapon.

My vision clears. Blood drips from my face to the carpet. I'm alone, brandishing a yellow umbrella. The computer is on, the screen displaying Google.

After my nosebleed is under control, I start a Discord call with Ash to give him a first-time streaming pep talk, and to see what kind of hardware we're dealing with on his end.

"Uh—you okay?" Ash says once his camera loads. His camera quality isn't the best, but I've seen worse. "What happened to your face?"

I jolt when I see myself on-screen. A bruise is forming on my nose, the bridge swollen, nostrils clogged with tissue. My hair is still all frizzed out everywhere. Definitely going to need a good flat ironing and makeup session before we go live.

"So I was sitting here and then"—I shudder, remembering the creepy whispering, the hand on my head—"there was a voice." I look at the little red dot of the webcam. The way I heard it speaking from my monitor, the fact that it latched on to me through a video game—I'm half convinced the thing lives inside the computer. What if it's always watching through the webcam? Is it even safe to talk about this stuff with Ash online? Will my computer ever be safe again? Dread twists in my stomach.

"And then what?" he asks.

"I got a nosebleed."

"You got a nosebleed that bruised your face?"

I clear my throat. "Emon-day lives in the omputer-cay," I say in choppy pig latin. "Possibly."

Ash blinks at me, taking a moment to process my words. "Umm. I think I get what you're . . . aying-say."

I nod. "Cool, do you have a lamp you can put on your desk? It'll help with lighting so the viewers can see you better."

"Ugh, I guess." Ash leans forward, moving things around.

"So the key to keeping the viewers entertained is to have a constant banter going, okay? Make sure you respond to what they're saying in the chat, but don't worry too much. I'll lead."

"Fine." Ash's video brightens, the lamp illuminating his face.

"That's better."

Ash gives a curt nod.

"We'll go live in an hour?"

"Guess so." The way he fidgets with his hands tells me he's nervous.

"It'll be okay, and I'm glad we're finally getting to do this . . . honey." I feel awkward AF saying that, but if the demon really is watching me from the computer, then I have to convince it that Ash is my little honeybunch.

I smile and widen my eyes at Ash, telling him to play along.

"Yeahhhh. Can't wait . . . babe." Ash looks down. "It's really hot when you . . . put that snake around your neck," he mumbles.

Ash knows about Bakugo? I guess he would if he's watched my streams before. "Yeah, he misses you. We both miss you," I say confidently, the awkwardness melting away as my Twitch persona extends to my fake-girlfriend act. I blow a kiss at the camera.

Ash blinks back at me, face crimson, smiling as if in pain. Why is he so embarrassed? It's just acting.

"Well, see you soon!" I say. "Love you!" I end the call before Ash spontaneously combusts from the shame.

An hour later, after I've concealed my nose with makeup,

straightened my hair, and gotten my phone back from Mom, I log in to Twitch. I've decided that Ash and I will play *The Forest* together, a horror game in which the survivors of a plane crash are stranded on an island inhabited by cannibals. It requires teamwork, and there's plenty going on for commentary. A perfect newbie streamer game.

Viewers start arriving as the game loads. A few dozen at first, and within a minute we're up to 100. Nowhere near the 800 to 1000 of my glory days—or the 1,200 the doppelgänger pulled in yesterday—but it's still a promising turnout.

"Hey, guys, I'm back with a special guest." I give a big smile to the camera. "Meet my boyfriend, Ash. We've been together a while now, but today's the first time I talked him into being on my channel."

"Hi." Ash gives a shy little wave.

Chat messages start rolling in:

cute

happy for you

sad day, Viv is taken

leave her alone

show us dem titties again viv

My face turns hot. Do they prefer the doppelgänger over the real me? We're up to 300 viewers now. Maybe they're only logging in because they're hoping it'll be her. I'd sound insane if I start telling them that the person they saw last night wasn't actually me, so what do I say?

"Vivian was trying something new yesterday," Ash says bluntly. "She'll game wearing whatever she wants, and today it's a *Pokémon* T-shirt." His tone is surprisingly scary when he's serious. I like the intensity.

"Yeah," I follow up, trying not to grin too obviously at how Ash just stood up for me. "Time to slaughter some cannibals."

Our characters spawn in the plane wreckage, suitcases and wiring strewn about the cabin.

"Take all the snacks!" I say to Ash. His avatar picks up the bags of chips and candy bars scattered around the seats.

don't forget the alcohol

get the axe!!

Ash and I each pick up an orange hatchet, then finish collecting the snacks, cloth, and everything grabbable. Once the plane is thoroughly looted, we find a clearing near a pond in the forest where we build a small cabin and eat a turtle for dinner.

As the sun sets, Ash and I lock ourselves in our cabin. Night falls, and soon, our screens are flashing red, screeches and high-pitched cackling coming from outside the door.

"Cannibals are here!" I say. "Run or fight?"

"Fight, duh." Ash lights a Molotov cocktail. I open the door and Ash throws the explosive at the cannibal shooting arrows. Behind us, the cabin wall breaks down and two bone club–wielding cannibals burst inside. Ash's character jumps behind me, taking the majority of the damage and fighting back with a stick.

"Just hold them off for a second!" I run to the charred cannibal outside and grab the bow and arrows, then headshot the cannibals in the shack.

omg

u two are so cute together

"We're lucky it was a small raid." I wrap Ash's character's wounds in alcohol and gauze.

this is love

nurse viv

I pan my camera across the dead cannibals while Ash loots their bodies, taking their teeth and weapons.

"You know what they say?" I start chopping up the corpses, collecting a pile of arms and legs.

"What?"

"An effigy a day keeps the cannibals away."

lol

yes

what are u going to make

I open the craft menu and begin building an effigy: stacking the legs and arms on a wooden pole so they bloom upward and out like a macabre bouquet. Ash adds a few feathers and fingers as a finishing touch.

"It's beautiful." I stand my character back to pan the camera around our work.

a work of art

won't keep the cannibals away for long

i'm sorry Viv

so sorry

Those last couple messages catch my attention. I glance away from the game to look at the username: GinnySnow. Where the hell has she been? And what could she possibly be apologizing about?

"Hey, Jen," I say, my bubbly Twitch persona masking my confusion. "Glad you're still around. Bet you hoped I'd never come back." I chuckle.

omg GinnySnow you're back?!

ur not welcome here

we stan for Viv!!!

"Jen can watch if she wants. Gotta keep an eye on what the competition's up to."

forgive me, GinnySnow types, then she stops responding.

Weird. What is she sorry for? One of my ideas she stole? She's never been remorseful before. But I don't have long to dwell on it—Ash is heading into a cave, and I descend into the darkness after him.

"Okay, I did your stupid stream," Ash says when I call after we log out. "Now what?"

I smirk, knowing full well he had fun.

"Now . . ." Ash and I should spy on the doppelgänger, recording it in the act of pretending to be me so we have hard evidence, but I don't want to say any of that out loud in case it can hear me. "I think I just want to come see you."

"Okay. I, uh . . . want to see you too," Ash says, playing along.

"So when can I come over?"

"Around ten? That's probably when my mom will pass out."

"Great, babe. See you soon." I make a smoochy kissing sound and hang up before I can feel his judgment radiating through the phone. But once the comfort of his presence on the other line disappears, I'm alone in my room again. My monitor goes into sleep mode. *Oh hell no.* I rattle the mouse and change the settings to Never Sleep.

I pace my room. Is this plan even a good one—hanging out and filming the demon? And then what? We find out where it goes and throw a net over it? I groan. It's either this or sit around and wait for it to do the next awful thing, and I'm definitely not doing that. I pack the iron dagger in my backpack, making sure I wrap it well in a T-shirt so I don't accidentally stab myself and bleed to death. Then I would definitely be trending as #tragedy.

I sit and wait until it's time to sneak out. This whole thing might be a stupid plan, maybe even a futile one, but it's the only one I've got.

THREE MONTHS AGO

Since Riley was allergic to almost all enjoyable food, the only dessert she could have was sorbet. The strawberry was her favorite. We sat at the counter, sharing a bowl, Riley singing a screeching song about "yummy bears" (berries). When she was done, the sorbet was somehow everywhere: the counter, the floor, her hands, face, legs, hair, and ears.

I helped her wash her hands in the sink, then carried her upstairs. She'd need a bath before our parents got home. In fact, they'd probably appreciate it if I had her ready for bed, and then they'd leave me alone so I could stream the rest of the night.

When I passed Riley's room, she squirmed in my arms, pushing her chubby little arms against me with surprising strength. "I wanna *play*." She craned her neck for the dollhouse in her room.

It'd be easier to get the bath set up without her anyway. "Fine, go ahead." I set her down and she ran off to her room.

In my parents' bathroom, I sat on the toilet while the tub filled, scrolling through Twitch on my phone. I swiped through the *What's Hot* livestreams, and there was GinnySnow, streaming *Morgue Mayhem*.

WTF.

I'm the one who discovered *Morgue Mayhem*, the new indie Korean horror game, and had streamed it two nights ago. Was GinnySnow so desperate for subscribers she was going to poach my content like I wouldn't notice? I opened the stream, watching GinnySnow's annoyingly shiny red hair and giggling face on my screen.

GinnySnow, her real name Jen, was a couple years older than me and went to University of Minnesota. We both started streaming around two years ago and gravitated toward the same types of games. We had a lot of follower overlap, which was naturally ripe for some friendly rivalry. But then Jen started getting really intense about it and spread rumors that I bought half my followers and am secretly a TERF—total bullshit and a desperate attempt to steal my following. It cost me a few hundred followers and a dozen subscribers. I got her back by spreading rumors that she cheats and uses aimbots. I even took a screenshot of one of her streams and photoshopped a watermark of auto-aim software into the background. Mean, yes. But she started it.

Jen's avatar ran up and down the halls of the morgue, a chainsaw-wielding doctor chasing after her. She missed the key in the janitor closet that was—hello—*glowing*, and had since been spending five minutes running around, trying doors to no avail. Yet, for some reason, people were still continuously logging in to watch her. Some generous soul, who probably knew where to find the key from *my* stream, told her what she'd missed in the chat.

The sound of rushing water stopped, snapping my attention back to the tub. It'd filled so high the faucet was submerged. I quickly turned the knob off and dipped my hand in to test the temperature. I yanked my hand back. Scalding hot. It'd need at least fifteen minutes or so to cool down. I went to Riley's room, where she was sitting on the floor, giggling and mashing two dolls together.

"You can play for fifteen more minutes, then it's bath time, okay?" I'm not sure she really had a great concept of time. It was more so a reminder for myself than her.

"Okee!"

Fifteen minutes. What if I logged in to *Morgue Mayhem* for that time? That's all I needed to show viewers that Jen was a miserable person with as much charm as a mollusk and I was the only horror streamer they needed in their lives.

I left Riley in her room and went to my gaming desk, where I smoothed my long blue braid off to the side, pulled a panda beanie over my head, then went live on Twitch.

A decision I would regret forever.

When I pull up to Ash's house, he's standing outside his apartment's front door.

I bound up the stairs. "Hey." I tell him my plan to film the doppelgänger.

"I like it. Come in." Ash opens the door, stepping into the dark living room. "Quietly."

"Isn't your mom home?" I whisper. "I thought we'd watch from across the street—"

"That's why I said *quietly*." He gestures for me to follow.

I step inside, holding my breath. It's so dark, Ash's figure is a shadow I can barely discern. I freeze, my heart rate steadily climbing. A sickening thought hits me: *What if this isn't Ash at all?* What if this is the doppelgänger luring me into a trap?

"Ash," I whisper. "It's really you, right?" I almost facepalm. What a stupid question to ask if he is, in fact, the doppelgänger.

"Um, yeah?" He stops moving and turns to me.

I step closer to see his face, studying the freckles on his nose, the patchy little hairs growing on his chin, the angled shape of his eyebrows. It's him. I'm 90 percent sure. Still, this thing was good enough at mimicry to trick my own parents, so I need to be 110 percent sure.

"What?" he whispers.

"Just paranoid."

"Okay, well, save it for when we're outside." He gestures toward the balcony door, tiptoeing for it. He gently opens the door and closes it silently behind us. "You're not scared of heights, right?"

"Kind of, yeah."

Ash puts one foot on the balcony railing and one hand on the window ledge.

My eyes widen. He wants me to scale a building, seriously? That's fun in *Assassin's Creed* games, but the real me stays firmly planted on the ground.

"It's totally safe," Ash says, now standing on the railing, balancing himself against the wall. "I've been doing this for years."

Ash kicks off the balcony, pulling himself up to the window

ledge, reaching for the roof siding. My pulse quickens. This does not look "totally safe." It's only a two-story building, so the fall won't kill me, but I definitely don't need a dislocated shoulder on top of everything else.

"Why do we even have to go up there?" I whisper-yell.

Ash hoists himself up from the window ledge to the roof in one smooth motion, making it look easy with his scrawny body. He lies on his stomach and bends down, reaching for me.

"So we can watch the doppelgänger from up high." He waves his hand impatiently. "Don't be a chicken. Just get on the railing, and then I'll pull you up myself."

I groan and step onto the railing, one hand steadying myself on the wall. I take Ash's hand, squeezing tightly, and kick off the balcony, reaching with my free hand for the window ledge.

Bang!

My knee bashes into the wall, rattling the window. Shit.

I wince, closing my eyes. Hopefully his mom didn't hear that. The last thing I need is her catching us and calling my parents. Then they'd have a real reason to be pissed at me. A moment of silence passes.

"Okay, come on," Ash hisses, tugging my arm. I kick off the window ledge. Ash grabs me under my armpits, which are tragically sweaty, and hoists me onto the roof.

I lie on my back for a moment, breathing heavily.

"You're seriously winded?" Ash says. "I did most of the work."

I playfully slap his arm. "Shut up."

He chuckles. "Follow me."

The building is L-shaped, and we walk toward the opposite end of the roof, hunched over like two characters in sneak mode.

"This is a good spot," Ash says when we reach the other side. He kneels, then splays down onto his stomach. "We'll just lay here flat, and watch."

I kneel beside him. From here, we have a clear shot of the parking lot and Ash's front door. It's perfect. I just wish we'd brought a blanket. It's still summer, but the roof's shingles have cooled in the night air.

"So." I lie down on my stomach beside Ash. "Why have you been coming onto the roof for years?" I raise my eyebrows.

"Cool place to smoke. Be alone. Wanted my own space after all the shit with my dad went down."

"Oh." I search for something else to say.

"You cold?"

"A little."

Ash scoots closer to me, his side warming mine. I look at his face, studying his warm brown eyes, the bump in the middle of the ridge of his nose, his long eyelashes. That little pimple between his eyebrows was there yesterday, but I still have to be sure he's not the doppelgänger.

"This is going to sound crazy, but I think it's warranted considering that we're literally spying on my evil doppelgänger.

We know this thing can make itself look like other people, or me at least, so how do you know I'm me? The real me? Like what if I'm the demon right now?"

"Oh, shit." Ash inches away from me. "Good point."

"I *am* the real me. But see? That's what I mean. And how do I know you're you? We don't know the extent of its powers."

Ash looks up, thinking. He pulls a pocketknife from his pants. "What if we make a little mark? Something small and hidden that only we know about?"

"Um, maybe?" I'm all for gory stuff, but pain? No thanks.

Ash takes my "maybe" as enough of an agreement. He flips the knife open and pushes the edge into his palm, a small slice once right, then left, not even flinching, like he's done this before. A few drops of blood dribble down his hand.

I wince. "Doesn't that hurt?"

"Nah."

He hands the knife to me. I hesitate. "What if it gets infected?"

Ash scoffs. "Don't wipe your ass with it. Plus, might even make your immune system stronger."

I take the knife, lining the edge up with the palm of my hand.

"Not too deep. I barely used any pressure."

"Okay." I stare at the middle of my hand.

"Want me to do it?"

"No, I got it." *Now isn't the time to wimp out. A little cut is nothing when there's a demon you need to take down.* I push the knife into palm and gasp. The sensation of my skin splitting is shocking but not exactly painful, like my hand's just been dipped into ice. I swipe the knife quickly the other way. Okay, now it's starting to hurt.

I give the knife back to Ash, clutching my bleeding hand closed. "We should have a passphrase too. Then with both the mark and a code word, we have two-step verification. For all we know the doppelgänger changes when I do, like if I got a tattoo it would appear on it too."

"Good point," Ash says. "What word?"

I rack my mind for a suitable word, but the first ones I think of—*bananas, chinchillas, spaghetti*—don't sound serious enough for the situation. "How about . . . *vermillion*?"

"What is that?"

"A shade of red. Heard it in *LOCKED IN*."

His eyes narrow. "The game where the demon found you in the first place?"

"Yeah." I turn my focus back to the front door. *Please don't ask about my secret again, don't ask don't ask don't ask.*

Ash is quiet, and we lie there in silence. It's a cloudy, starless night, the moon a thin sliver between the fluffy clouds. A few minutes pass, then a few more. My mind wanders to Riley, like it always does when I'm not filling it with something else.

I remember how one night a few weeks before she died, she reached for the sunscreen and pointed at the moon while saying "moonburn," thinking it could burn her skin like the sun. The memory makes me smile, and then I think of the horrible things I did, how her body was so pale, so small and fragile. My stomach twists into a hot, aching knot.

I look at Ash. "Can I ask you something?"

"Hmm?"

"How'd you get over it? Your dad."

Ash sweeps the hair out of his eyes. "Guess I'm not really over it. I just live with it."

"Do you two talk at all?"

"Yeah. He writes and calls every week."

"Oh." I couldn't even imagine having that sort of long-distance relationship with one of my parents. "And you . . . write back?"

"Of course. I send him my drawings and stuff. We exchange book recs."

"So you're not, like, still . . . mad at him? For what he did?"

Ash bristles.

"Sorry if I'm asking too much. People gossip in this town, and I guess I just wanted to know how you feel about it." *Oh my god, Viv, shut up. Leave the poor boy and his trauma alone!* "So, you watch any anime?" I say quickly, trying to change the conversation.

"It's okay," Ash says. "I was mad, yeah. It was hard to accept what he'd done, but . . ." Ash shrugs. "People fuck up. I know he regrets it, and he's still my dad."

I don't know what to say back. I just nod.

"But it's still tough. There are days when I still blame myself," Ash continues.

"Wait, what?" I prop myself up on my elbow. "How? You were just a kid. You weren't even there."

Ash rolls his eyes. "That's what everyone says. But I knew my dad had a drinking problem. I could've taken his keys. I could've warned someone."

I shake my head. "It wasn't your fault. That's just what-if thinking. We all have those thoughts." I can't help but feel agitated—Ash was literally a victim in this. I *actually* did something terrible. My actions directly caused Riley's death. He doesn't know what it's like to blame yourself and really deserve it.

"You okay?" Ash asks.

"Yeah, I just . . ." I trail off, the thought hitting me that I could tell Ash. I could tell the whole horrible secret to him, how I killed Riley, all the lies I've told since to cover it up. And then what? What would that change? Nothing. I can never undo what happened, and I can't risk him learning what a terrible person I am. We've just become friends, and I can't lose him too. Still, I ache to unburden myself.

"I had a friend once." I look away from Ash. "Who did something terrible. She . . . got the family dog killed."

"Damn, that sucks."

"Yeah, but then she made it look like an accident so no one would know it was her fault. And then she never told anyone because everyone would hate her if they found out what she did."

Ash is quiet for a moment. "That'd be a fucked-up burden to carry."

"I know, right," I whisper. "It ate her up inside. Every day." I let my hair fall so Ash can't see the tears welling in my eyes. "But she was just a friend," I say, trying to sound nonchalant. "And it was a long time ago. I'd practically forgotten about it."

Ash puts his arm around my shoulders. I can't tell if this is a comforting gesture over my made-up friend's sob story or part of our act to seem like a couple. I lean into his warmth, and for the few minutes we lie there like that, some of the pain fades.

"How'd the dog die?" Ash asks.

"What?"

"Your friend's dog?" Ash cocks one eyebrow.

"Oh, yeah. Umm . . ." I stall. "I don't know. I think she fed it something it wasn't supposed to eat." A flash of pink moves in the corner of my eye. My breath hitches. There's a girl skipping through the parking lot wearing a pink hoodie—*my* pink Kirby hoodie—and an old pair of jeans and converse, a greenish-gray side ponytail poking out from beneath the hood. No one else has that ugly ass hair. No one other than me.

Ash's grip tightens on my shoulder. "You're here."

Ash whips out his phone and starts recording. I crawl closer to the edge of the roof. My doppelgänger heads for the stairs to Ash's apartment. With the hoodie propped up over its head and the darkness, it's hard to tell that it looks like me, definitely not enough to convince anyone.

"Zoom in," I say to Ash. "You need a clear shot of its face." But instead of filming the doppelgänger, Ash points the camera toward me.

"What are you doing?"

"It doesn't do any good to show you just down there. I have to prove that you're in two places at once."

I smile. Smart. "Yeah, I totally thought of that too." I lean against Ash, watching the footage over his arm. It's still too dark.

"Can you get closer? We need better lighting."

"I'm trying." Ash scoots toward the roof's edge.

The doppelgänger walks up the stairs, moving in quick, jerking movements, like it's glitching forward. Perfect. No human walks like that. I can't help but smile at the thought of showing this footage to Bri and my parents and them forgiving me. Then they'll all ask for *my* forgiveness for not believing me in the first place.

Ash follows the doppelgänger with his phone as it approaches the door. "I still can't get your face clearly. Maybe if I just—" The flash on Ash's phone turns on. "Oh shit."

We both scramble back, pressing ourselves down. My blood pressure spikes. The light on Ash's phone turns off.

"Does it know we're here?" I whisper.

Ash is still holding the phone up, but has his head down. "It looked this way for a second," he says, a slight tremble in his voice. "But now it seems focused on the apartment again."

I glance over the edge of the roof. The doppelgänger's facing the door. It tries the handle, jiggling it. Locked. How's it going to get inside?

The doppelgänger presses its hands to the wall, like it's searching for a door that's not there. I cover my mouth as I watch myself—pink hoodie, pants, body, and all—fade to black. A gaunt, shadowy figure stands on the railing. It's hunched over, thin arms unnaturally long, hanging down to its knees. The fingers extend out into long points. I reflexively touch the scabs on my arm. The demon steps forward, disappearing through the wall. I gasp, my heart drumming in my chest.

"Oh my god. Did you get that on video?"

"Hell yeah I did." Ash holds the phone with both hands to keep it from shaking too much.

"What do you think it's doing in there?"

"I don't know. You don't think it's in there, like, killing my mom or something, right?" He looks at me, worried.

"No," I whisper. At least I hope not. I really couldn't live with myself then. "It probably went in there to break up with you as me or something." I gnaw my thumb nail. What *is* it doing in there? It should've noticed we're not there by now. "Should we go in?"

Ash shifts uncomfortably. "Another minute?"

"Yeah."

"Look!" Ash whispers. The demon steps out the way it came in, its small orange eyes glowing in the night. Halfway down the stairs, its dark form morphs back into me with the pink hoodie. Its hunched-over, animalistic steps turn into skips, and it disappears into the night.

I let out a long breath. "Jesus Christ."

Ash ends the recording. "We got it. Already emailed it to you."

"Upload it to the cloud in case the doppelgänger tries to delete it or something."

Ash presses a few buttons on his phone. "Done."

"Show me the video. I want to make sure this will really work." Did we really outsmart it this easily? It feels too good to be true.

Ash holds the phone in front of us and presses play. The quality isn't great, but the girl in the parking lot looks just like me, especially if you pause and zoom in. The cheekbones, the eyebrows, the hair. It's unmistakably me. The video continues, even showing the part where it dissolved from me into a dark shadow form. The transformation could be argued as CGI, but it will be enough for Mom, Dad, and Bri to finally believe me. I smile, my eyes watering from relief. This is going to work.

"Thanks Ash. We really did it."

"No prob. Now what?"

"I'll show it to my parents and explain the whole thing to them. Same with Bri. And then . . . if we lured the doppelgänger here, I'm sure we can do it again. And this time, we'll have a plan to get rid of it for good." I think of the knife in my backpack. If the thing can walk through walls, can I even stab it to death? I don't know, but if I have my friends and family on my side again, together we'll come up with something.

Ash studies the worry on my face. "We'll think of a plan. All things can die. Even demons."

I nod. "I guess I should go home now. Thanks for the help."

"Yeah. Of course."

But neither of us moves. We stay on the roof, side-by-side. Ash's arm trembles against mine.

"You okay?" I ask.

"I'm good."

"Really? I can feel you shaking."

He snickers. "Just haven't had a smoke in a while."

"Uh-huh."

"If I'm being honest, I am a little freaked out by how it just went into my house like that."

"Me too." I shudder. "It's been in my house too. In my room."

"Stay for a little while?" Ash shifts to look me in the eyes, his gaze so intense I have to glance away. "Maybe you can show me one of those animes you're so in to."

"Yeah." I smile. "That'd be nice."

We sneak along the roof the way we came, climbing quietly back onto the balcony, the way down much easier than the way up. I follow Ash into the apartment, tiptoeing behind him to his room. He shuts the door behind us and turns on the lights. I cover my mouth, holding back a scream.

Ash's eyes widen. "Holy shit."

Written in red across Ash's wall are the words:

I SEE EVERYTHING

I HEAR EVERYTHING

I AM EVERYWHERE

"Oh shit. You think that's, like, literal?" My pulse skyrockets.

I look around to make sure the demon isn't crouched in the closet or hanging upside down on the ceiling.

"I don't know." Ash scratches at the words. "Maybe it saw us? Maybe . . . it can read your mind."

My blood runs cold. "Don't say that!" If it can read my mind, then it'll always be ten steps ahead of me. It'll be impossible to stop. I sit on his bed, putting my head between my knees, my fingers going numb from anxiety.

Ash puts his hand on my shoulder. "Actually, it needed to read your journals and stuff, so I really doubt it can read your mind. It was a dumb comment, sorry."

My panic soothes a little. Still, this is all too much. The doppelgänger knew what we were up to. What terrible thing is it plotting next? I wrap my arms around myself, my stomach twisting.

"Ash, I'm like—" I hate the tremble in my voice. "Really scared."

He sits beside me. "Me too."

"What do you think it's going to do now that it knows we're onto it?" I think about what Addison said: *Kill it before it kills you.* "What if it's going to kill and replace me?" My throat tightens. "My Twitch followers believed it was me. My own parents didn't even notice when it ate dinner with them the other night. This thing could totally off me and just slip right into my life—"

"I won't let it." Ash takes my hand, the one that's crusted

with blood. It stings, but I still clutch on to him. "And if you don't want to be alone tonight, you can stay here."

"I can't—" I start, but then I think about driving home, sitting in the car alone, then going to my dark house where my parents are asleep, oblivious, and up to my bedroom with my computer. I touch my nose that's still tender. I shiver.

I never want to be alone again.

"Okay, I'll stay." If my parents are pissed at me now, they might combust with rage if they discover that I snuck out and didn't come home, but they sleep in on Saturdays. I'll go home when the sun rises, before Mom and Dad wake.

Ash stands. "You take the bed. I'll sleep on the floor—"

"No." I pull his hand back toward me. "Just stay close."

"Uh, okay." Ash glances down, lips pursed.

I lie on his bed, my hair fanning around me. Ash lies next to me, his arm and leg warm against mine. His bed is surprisingly comfortable, and I feel safe next to him, safer than I've felt in so many nights. The pounding in my chest slows, the tightness around my ribs easing. My breathing grows from shallow and quick to slow and regular.

"Vivian?" Ash says, his voice heavy with sleepiness.

"Hmm?"

"The gossip you mentioned earlier about me and my dad . . . what do they say?"

My eyes flutter open. My mouth dries. *They say you're crazy, smelly, murderous, satanic, likely to end up in prison like your dad. I've said those things too.* "Dumb stuff. Don't worry about it."

"I heard people saying that I collect dead opossums."

My stomach twists. *I* was the one who said that. But in my defense, I did see him pick one up. "Someone said they saw you picking one up. You didn't?" I wait for him to lie to me.

"I do," he says. "I keep a pair of rubber gloves in my car just so I can check their pouches for babies. My dad taught me to do that when I was younger. Once, we found a dead female with a whole litter in her pouch, helpless little babies cold and starving. We warmed them up and took them to a wildlife rehabilitator."

A lump grows in my throat. That's the goddamn sweetest thing I've ever heard. And I told people that he collects dead opossums to do satanic rituals with them. What the hell is wrong with me? "Some asshole said that." I squeeze his hand, vowing to never say a bad word about him again. "Don't worry about it."

I rest my head against his arm, drifting into my first nightmare-free sleep in weeks.

When I wake, I'm lying on my side, Ash's arm draped around my waist. He's snoring softly. I close my eyes again. It's so warm snuggled up like this with him. If only it weren't for the sunlight beaming right into my face, I could fall back to sleep.

Wait. Sunlight.

I bolt upright, knocking Ash's arm off me. "What time is it?"

I climb over him and stand, frantically stepping into my shoes.

"Shit." Ash sits up, feeling around for his phone. "Seven thirty."

"I have to leave right now!" Mom and Dad might still be in bed. "Can I go out the front door or—?" I stand beside Ash, bouncing on my feet in a little panic dance.

Ash ducks into the hallway. A toilet flushes from the bathroom.

"Go now!" He waves his hand for me to hurry past him.

I dart down the hallway and outside. Damn it, I really have to pee, but there's no time. I sprint to my car and start the drive home, careful not to go more than five miles an hour over the speed limit, so I don't risk getting pulled over. I get stuck at two red lights. *Shit shit shit.* I grip the steering wheel, squeezing the life out of it, and gun it forward once the light turns green.

One more intersection until I turn onto my street. Of course, this one traps me at another freaking red light. It turns green, but the silver Honda Odyssey in front of me doesn't move.

"GO LADY!" I scream, honking the horn.

The van slowly rolls forward. I step on the gas. "Come on, come on." If there is a god, Mom and Dad will still be asleep, but in case they're up, I rack my brain for a way to explain my absence. I rummage through the trash on the passenger-side floor, picking up an old caramel macchiato cup.

"Just went out for Starbucks!" I practice saying. I'll walk in with this, sipping like it's full. It'll be fine. Totally fine. Just in case, I rip off the mobile order sticker dated from five days ago. I take the fastest right turn of my life onto my street and nearly pee my pants.

In my driveway are two cop cars, lights flashing.

THREE MONTHS AGO

"Hey, hey, hey!" I said as viewers started logging in. "Ready to bash some brains in this murder morgue?"

As more viewers signed on, I didn't waste any time with giggling and fluff like GinnySnow. These people wanted to see me kill zombies, and that I would do. I picked up a scalpel and rammed it into the eye of a rabid med student, repeatedly. There wasn't much in terms of story in this game, but plenty of gore and inventive ways to get kills, which viewers love. I had GinnySnow's stream open on my phone to keep an eye on her viewer count, and with each kill, my viewer number was catching up to hers.

After decapitating the zombified doctor by ramming his head with the morgue freezer door, my viewer count surpassed Jen's, and I was swept up in that streamer high: a glowing, floating, invigorating warmth. Another tier-two subscriber joined my channel. A grin spread across my face. That'd be another five dollars in my bank account. I really could make this a career.

I flung a hacksaw at an undead med student in the hallway,

sending the chat cheering with messages of headshot FTW!!!!

I didn't want to stop playing, but the bath water was probably a good temperature by now. Any longer and it might get too cold. "I have to go guys, but I'll try to log back in soon." I blew a kiss at the screen and took my headset off, then looked at the time on my phone. 2:09 p.m. *What?*

I'd been playing for forty-five minutes. *Shit.* The bath water was definitely too cold now, and I shouldn't have left Riley alone this long. What if she made a mess while I was distracted? Or got into the pantry and ate something she wasn't supposed to?

I rushed to her bedroom, throwing the door open. She wasn't there. *Shit shit shit.*

"Riley?" I called over the staircase in case she'd gone back to the kitchen. No answer. I ran down the stairs, fearing I'd find her swollen and covered in hives while eating the forbidden cheese she was always trying to get into. Not here either.

"Riley?!" I called, my voice growing shrill as my stress grew. "Where are you?"

I checked the pantry, the cabinet under the sink, the linen closet. Riley had thought spontaneous hide-and-seek was funny before, so it was reasonable to assume she was just holed up somewhere. Still, I felt sick with the idea that something bad had happened.

I inhaled. Exhaled.

Think logically. She had to be in the bathroom—*duh.* My

mind had been buzzing with so much panic, I hadn't even thought of the most obvious place to look. She was probably waiting for me to get her into the bath.

I ran upstairs and through my parent's room. "Rye—you ready for that bath?" I halted to a stop in the bathroom. My heart lurched.

No.

This couldn't be happening.

Riley was in the bathtub. Floating.

Face down.

Blood pounds in my ears. Mom and Dad must've woken to find me not in my bed and reported me missing. *Oh shit oh shit oh shit.* I park my car and run up the driveway, clutching the old Starbucks cup like it might still help somehow.

"I'm okay, Mom!" I yell as I run into the kitchen. "I'm not missing!"

I come to a full stop, my stomach plummeting. The old coffee cup drops from my hand.

Two policemen are in the kitchen. One's talking to Mom, who's dabbing her eyes with a tissue, and the other is putting handcuffs on Dad. What the fuck is going on?

Dad's face crumples when he sees me. His legs weaken and the officer holds him up by his arms pinned behind his back. "Viv, how could you say I did those things? All because of—" His voice cracks, his face twisting. "TwitchCon?"

"*What?*" I ask, my voice coming out in a strained squeak. "What are you talking about? This must be a mistake—"

I go to Dad, putting a hand on his shoulder. "Take these cuffs off him!" I say to the cop. "Why are you doing this?" My voice sputters as I start to cry.

The other cop steps in front of me. He's tall, white, no older than thirty, with a patchy brown beard. The badge on his chest reads Officer Jones. "Young lady, we understand that you're a victim here, but it's very serious to file a report and then run away from us."

"*What?* I never filed any report—" A wave of nauseating realization hits me. My doppelgänger did this. "I swear, that wasn't me."

"Oh really? Because I'm the one who just saw you—" Officer Jones starts, but I'm already running away from him to Mom.

"Mom, I need my phone. Now."

She's wearing her light blue robe, leaning against the kitchen counter, talking on the phone. She puts a hand up to quiet me.

"Please, Mom!" My voice rises. "Give me my phone. It's to help Dad." I put a hand on her arm, squeezing with urgency.

I need to show the video to the cops and prove that the report was bullshit.

"Hold on a second." She yanks the phone away from her ear. "I'm speaking with a lawyer to get your father out of this mess. This is not the time." She glares at me, her eyes daggers.

"Dad's innocent! I can prove it—"

"I know he's innocent," Mom says, her voice harsher than I've ever heard before. She turns back to the phone. "Hi, sorry about that—"

I pivot, running up the stairs to her room. My phone has to be in there somewhere.

I burst through the bedroom door, my chest tight with panic. Air, I need air. I inhale through my nostrils and slowly exhale, throwing open Mom's dresser drawers. *It's going to be okay*. I'll find my phone and show the officers that I have a doppelgänger running around spewing lies as me, then Dad will be freed.

I go through the dresser, finding only clothes. Where's the freaking phone? It doesn't help that I can hardly see from the tears and snot seeping from my face. I yank open the drawer of the nightstand, pulling it and all the contents to the floor. My phone tumbles onto my foot. I grab it and sprint downstairs.

Dad and the police aren't in the kitchen anymore. Shit.

"Vivian—" Mom starts as I fly past her and out the front door.

The other policeman opens the car door while Officer Jones guides Dad into the back seat.

"WAIT!" I run to Jones, holding my phone up. "I have proof!"

He shuts the door on Dad, locking him in the back of the police car.

"What is it?" the officer asks, eyebrows raised.

"Whatever you think I said about my dad—I didn't, I swear. I know it sounds crazy, but there's someone who looks exactly like me trying to ruin my life. Just watch this." I open the email on my phone, trying not to drop it with my trembling hands.

Officer Jones says nothing, just stares at me incredulously. I navigate to my email and click on the video Ash sent, holding it up for the officer to see.

The video plays, the camera panning from me sitting beside Ash to the balcony below. My doppelgänger creeps up the stairs, wearing the pink hoodie. The camera zooms in and it's hard to see—but the face, the grayish-green hair peeking out from the hood, it's unmistakably me. I pause and zoom in closer.

"See?! That's me down there, but I was sitting on the roof!"

The cop's face shifts from annoyance to intrigue. My hopes rise. *This is going to work.*

"Just keep watching." I press play again so the officer can see the doppelgänger's weird jerky movements up the stairs and how it passed through the wall. Then he'll have to let Dad go.

The doppelgänger takes its first step up the stairs, then the footage crackles, black and gray pixels engulfing the screen.

"No, no, no." I pause the video to try to get it to buffer. I start it again, but it's still pixelated, and when the video should be showing the demon's inhuman movements, the screen completely statics out. This can't be happening. The video was perfect last night.

The officer shifts his weight. "Look, we don't have time for pranks—"

"It's not a prank!" I yell, maybe too loudly. "Please, just wait."

The video comes into focus again, showing the doppelgänger facing the apartment. *Please, let this part work.* The doppelgänger turns directly toward the camera, a shit-eating grin spreads across its face. Then the whole video turns to black. *No.* I try refreshing, try rewinding and playing forward. Nothing. The rest of the footage is just a black screen.

I clench the phone and scream, "GODDAMN IT!"

Officer Jones's eyes widen, his face grimacing in a *This girl is insane* expression. "A case worker will be seeing you shortly." He opens the driver door and steps into the car.

"No, no, no. Don't go!" I rewind the video to the first part, pausing on the doppelgänger. "Look, that's me. A doppelgänger of *me*!"

Officer Jones hesitates, glancing at my phone warily. "The

case worker will be able to recommend mental health services to you."

I drop to my knees on the driveway as they take my dad away. The collar of his shirt is flipped up all wrong, his thinning hair a mess. He looks so small in the back of the cop car, so helpless.

A Gmail notification pops up on my phone, sent to me from my own email. My breathing stops as I tap it open.

Do you want to keep playing? Or are you ready to give up yet?

I pace my bedroom, hands shaking as I text Ash about how my dad just got arrested. I hope it's not too triggering for Ash, but if anyone would get what it's like to have your dad ripped from you by the police, it's him.

Ash: wtf??? i'm so sorry. we'll figure something out

Me: is your video of the doppelganger all pixelated too

Ash: let me check

Ash: shit. yeah it is

Me: fuuuuuck. what now?!

Ash: let me think. we'll get your dad out of this

I clutch the phone to my chest. How would I have ever gotten through this whole shit show without Ash's support? I wouldn't. I would've given up by now, melted into a slushy pile of depression.

"Vivian!" Mom yells. "Downstairs, now!"

I walk to the kitchen, too numb to feel any more panic. A Black woman with short, cropped hair and glasses stands by the fridge, holding a leather messenger bag at her hip.

"Hi, Vivian, I'm Kathy, your social worker." Her voice is serious but sweet. "I'm here to talk with you about your home life." She smiles politely at Mom. "Cheryl, if you could give us the room."

Mom nods and walks upstairs.

Kathy sits across from me at the kitchen table. She starts with basic questions: how was my summer, how's school, how's my social life.

"Awful," I deadpan.

She nods. "I understand you've had an issue with acting out recently. You made a threat to harm your ex-boyfriend and his friends?" Her tone is mostly pitying with a dash of judgment.

"Uh-huh." I don't have it in me to explain for the thousandth time that I was framed.

"Acting out is a normal response for victims in your situation."

"What situation?!" I pull on my own hair in frustration. "My dad hasn't done anything."

Kathy folds her hands together. "When did he first start getting violent?"

"*What?* He never has been."

Kathy peers at me from over her half-moon glasses. "It's okay, sweetie. Whatever you tell me is confidential."

"He's never hit me or anything, I swear."

Kathy frowns. "Earlier this morning, you walked into the police station and filed a report which stated," she quotes from her laptop, "'My name's Vivian Reynolds. We live at 221 Rose Street. I'm here to report a case of child abuse. My father is controlling and abusive and hits me when he thinks I've disobeyed him. He doesn't let me leave the house, and I'm scared of what he'll do to me next. A few months ago, he smothered my baby sister with a pillow and then made it look like an accident.'"

What the hell? I cover my mouth, too stunned to speak. That's low, even for a demon.

"The officer then took photos of your injuries," Kathy continues. "They were going to escort you home, but you disappeared from the station."

"Can I see the photos?"

She pulls one out of her manilla folder, showing me an image of myself with a black eye, swollen nose, and busted lip. It's startling seeing myself all beaten up. The doppelgänger must've bashed herself in the face to cause those injuries.

"Do you see any bruises on me?" I ask. "No! Because the whole thing's a lie!"

Kathy's face fills with pity. "Your nose looks swollen and bruised."

God damn it. I forgot that the demon smashed my face into the desk yesterday. "That was from something else!"

Kathy's voice softens. "You don't have to lie for him—"

"I'm NOT!" I point at the picture. "What about these other injuries? I don't have a black eye!"

"Are you wearing makeup?"

"Nope!" I leap from the chair and run water from the sink, splashing it on my face and rubbing it aggressively with a towel. "See?!"

Kathy cocks her head to the side, studying me, one eyebrow raised. "So, you're telling me"—the softness in her voice begins to harden—"that you filed a false report this morning?"

My stomach knots. Maybe the doppelgänger's plan wasn't just to get Dad thrown in prison but to also make me look like a pathological liar.

I bite my lip. She's never going to believe me if I say, "My doppelgänger did it," so if I want to free my dad, this is the only way how. "Yes." I look down. "I lied."

"And why would you do that?" Kathy says, her voice icy.

"I don't know. For attention? I thought it'd help me boost my followers." I twist the damp kitchen towel in my hands, racking my brain for a way to sell this story. "People would pity me, and they'd subscribe to my channel."

Kathy's lips curl in disgust. "You filed a false report to gain more . . . *followers*?"

"Yeah. And I was mad at him for not letting me go to TwitchCon." I sound like such a stupid brat, but I don't even care. I just have to save him. "I didn't think he would actually get arrested."

"You accused your father of *abuse* and *murder*, and didn't think anything would come of it?" Kathy's standing now, hands splayed on the table.

"He wasn't even here when Riley died—my parents were at a play in Chicago! My mom can show you the receipts."

Kathy scribbles a quick couple sentences. "I'll be speaking to your mother now. You can go." She waves her hand like I'm a swarm of flies she's shooing away.

I walk upstairs. Mom's pacing the hallway, arms wrapped tightly across her chest, her face red and blotchy.

"She wants to talk to you now. Mom, I didn't—" I hesitate. I want to tell her I didn't do this, but until I have actual proof of the doppelgänger, she's not going to believe me. "I'd never want to hurt you or Dad."

"When you were acting up this morning, I never imagined this was what you had planned," Mom says, her voice hoarse and fatigued. "I know you and your father disagree sometimes, but how could you do something like this?"

"What did I say this morning, exactly?"

She looks at me, bewildered. "You asked how long we were going to keep controlling and punishing you. You called us 'oppressive' and stormed out." Mom shakes her head. "We've been so lenient with you and then you go and do this?"

I swallow the knot in my throat. Last year, when Mom said Dad was right and we couldn't go to TwitchCon, I was furious, but I would never actually do something to hurt them. I settled for posting a rant about it on my channel; the doppelgänger must've watched it. I stammer for an explanation, but there's nothing to say. I glance away, Mom's reddened, swollen eyes too much for me to bear. I haven't seen her like this since Riley died.

Mom takes in a shaky breath. "You've destroyed this family, Vivian."

I cover my mouth, tears pooling between my fingers. She's right about that. I rush into my room and scream into my pillow. My "confession" that I made the whole thing up better get Dad released, or I don't know what I'll do.

My phone chimes. I hold it up to see a text from Bri. A brief smile flickers across my face. I've missed seeing her name on my phone.

Brianna: are you ok??? my mom said Betty called and said she saw your dad getting arrested. what happened??

I glance out the window at Betty's house, and sure enough, she's clutching a mug and watching through the curtains of her kitchen window like we're her own personal reality TV show. I shake my head.

Me: yeah. it's so fucked up. don't even know where to begin. i know it sounds crazy but the person doing these things—the sexts to Eric, the Tristan thing, getting my dad arrested. IT'S NOT ME

Three dots appear and disappear a few times, then my phone starts ringing.

I answer Bri's call. "Hey."

"I didn't know how to text this. I don't even know what I'm saying." She pauses. "But maybe I should've listened to you when you said someone's ruining your life."

My chest rises with hope.

"The police talked to me about the screenshots, and I would've remembered if you'd said crazy shit about killing Tristan. I told them those messages were fake."

"You didn't get in trouble, right?"

"No."

"Good."

"And then you showed up on my front door the other day and something felt . . . off. Your energy, how you were standing, you were way too stiff. Literally standing and staring at me like a creepy mannequin."

"And what did I want?" I throw a towel over the desktop monitor, paranoid that the doppelgänger's watching me. But even that's not enough to make me feel safe. I bound down the stairs and out to the front yard, standing barefoot in the grass.

"You were apologizing about the sexts sent to Eric, and you really wanted to come inside. Something was giving me major red flags, and I thought about what you said, about how there's someone who looks just like you doing all these bad things, and so I said, 'Hey, remember how we first met? We were at the mall, and you said you loved my top.' You nodded and said the shirt was super cute. But Viv, that's *not* how we met. I said I was busy and locked the door."

My stomach tightens. Thank god Bri is smart. What would it have done if she'd let it in? "We met in Mrs. Burns's sixth grade science class. I only had pens that day, not pencils, which she was so anal about, and you lent me a pencil. I remember because it was a mechanical one with 2.0 millimeter lead, and I cracked a joke about how you must have an iron grip to need lead that thick."

"Exactly. So why did you fall for my fake mall story when you came here?"

"Because it wasn't me. I swear. I swear on"—I press my hand to my chest—"Riley's soul that it was not me."

Bri's quiet for a moment. "This goes against every fiber of my being, but I think I believe you."

I gasp with relief. "Yes. Thank you. I know it's the wildest thing imaginable, but I swear I'd never betray you—"

"I know. I'm sorry I thought you did at first. I was such a bitch." Her voice is heavy with emotion. I can tell she genuinely regrets it, but there's no need. I already forgive her.

"It's okay. I wouldn't have believed it either. Look, you need to remember the word *vermillion*, okay? That's our password so we know one of us isn't the doppelgänger. *Vermillion.* Write it down. *Wait*, don't write it down. Too risky. Just remember it."

"Vermillion, got it. When you say 'our' password, you mean you and Ash?"

"Yeah."

"So . . . you two really are dating?"

"Let's just meet in person?" I don't know how, if, or when the doppelgänger's listening in on me, but it seems safer to be overly cautious. And really, I would love to be anywhere other than here, especially if I can see Bri. "I'm grounded but Mom might appreciate me not being here since she can't stand my existence right now."

"Yeah. Come over."

I hang up, and even though everything's still a shitstorm, I feel better with Bri back on my side. I go into the house. Mom's blowing her nose at the kitchen table, Kathy consolingly patting her shoulder. I bet I've made Kathy's top five worst children list. They glance at me, Kathy's eyes cold and steely, Mom's shining with tears and pain. My heart clenches.

I rush up the stairs and and leave a note for Mom: "Going to Bri's. I'm so sorry about all of this." Before I leave, I change out Bakugo's water bowl. Evil doppelgänger destroying my life is no excuse to slack on my snake mom duties.

I text Bri: OMW!!

I text Ash: meet me at Bri's. 319 Houston Ave

Ash: kk. you guys made up?

Me: yeah 😌

Ash: good

I pick up my backpack, double-checking the iron knife is still in there. My phone chimes from a series of Snapchat notifications. What now? I swipe it open, read the messages, and cover my mouth.

GinnySnow, my old gaming nemesis, is dead. She killed herself.

How much tragedy can happen in one summer? Hell, in one day?

I haven't even seen GinnySnow online since I've made my return, other than when she popped into my stream with Ash to say she was sorry. That hits way different now—sorry for *what*? Did she know she was going to kill herself then? And why would I matter in her last moments?

I sit on my bed, reading GinnySnow's final Instagram post. It's a screenshot of a farewell letter, typed in her notes app. The first two paragraphs talk about her love for her mom and brother, and she asks them to look after her pet ferrets, Mochi and Miso. My eyes mist reading the words. I barely knew Jen. Really, I only knew her Twitch persona, so in a way, I didn't know her at all. But she was another gamer. Only a couple years older than me. I can't believe things got so bad she resorted to this.

I read the next paragraph and pause on these words:

Those awful things I did, it wasn't me. I know I'll be forever remembered as crazy for saying this but something evil that looked like me caused so much pain to those I love. My greatest regret is that I passed this on to someone else. Forgive me.

My heart thumps in my chest. *What the hell?* I stand, reading those words again and again, making sure I'm not just making them up. *Something evil that looked like me.*

Could Jen have gone through the same thing I am?

I scroll through her past posts, going all the way back to midsummer. She posted a pic of herself, the caption: NOT ME NOT ME NOT ME—someone is trying to ruin my life!

I open the comments.

omg stop

such an attention whore

yeahhhh right

How did I not see this before? I look at the date of the picture. July 1. Riley died the first week of June. When Jen posted this, I was bundled up in bed, sleeping fourteen hours a day. If I got on the internet, it was to watch Netflix. For weeks, I didn't go on social media at all.

My hands tremble as I link the posts in a group text to Bri and Ash.

Me: guys i think GinnySnow went through the same thing i did. Remember her Bri??

Brianna: yah. can't believe she died. WDYM she went through the same thing

Me: she also had a doppelganger

Ash: whoa this letter is crazy. Viv, this could really help us figure this whole thing out

Brianna: ok Viv having an evil twin is hard enough to believe but now you think GinnySnow had one too??

Me: kind of yeah???

I go back to Instagram, scrolling through Jen's page. Does this mean she also played *LOCKED IN*?

June 21, she made a reel of herself wearing black lipstick, a creepy piano tune playing in the background. Her camera pans to the computer. LOCKED IN: An Escape Room Horror Game. The caption: New stream tonight!!!! Be sure to tune in!!! You're going to love this spooky game!!!

My hands clench the phone, sweat beading on my brow. I keep scrolling, but like I suspected—everything before the game is normal. Subathon promotions. Cosplays. Streaming clips. It's from the first day she played the game onward that things get weird.

I screenshot Jen's post about *LOCKED IN*, sending it to the group text.

She played the game too.

The three of us sit at the long wooden table in the den at Bri's house, lo-fi focus music playing softly from Bri's laptop. Ash scrolls through GinnySnow's social media accounts, taking notes.

"I know he's your fake BF," Bri whispers, leaning close to me. "But you had to bring creeper to my house?"

Ash doesn't flinch, but I know he heard that, and I'm not letting it fly a second longer.

"Let's get something straight—Ash might give off some different vibes." I pause to look at him. I have to admit he does seem out of place wearing his stitched up, pentagram labeled black vest in Bri's regal wood-paneled den, but I like that he's eccentric. "It's part of his goth boy aesthetic. It doesn't make him a 'creeper.'"

Bri rolls her eyes.

"And the rumors about him, they're just that. I've been in his room. He doesn't collect opossums or have a school shooting manifesto or whatever they say about him."

Ash's neck reddens.

Bri's eyes narrow at me. I know what she's thinking: *I'm* the one who started the opossum rumor. I'm the one who labeled him the "school shooter." If I were ever going to come clean about it, now's the perfect time. But I don't want to admit any of that, and why should I when I can just pretend it never happened? I'll make it up to Ash by being extra nice to him now. "And Ash is the only one who's been helping me during my crisis."

Bri's face softens at that. "I know. . . . Thanks for helping Viv out," she mumbles to Ash, then turns back to me. "So, if it's true that this game is what links you and Jen to the doppelgänger—which I still think is bonkers by the way—then I guess we could start with figuring out a timeline? What date did you first play the game?"

"The day of Mason's party, August twentieth."

Bri writes that down on her yellow legal pad.

"How'd you hear about the game in the first place?" Ash asks.

"It was emailed to me. From this." I show him the email on my phone. "There's no name."

"Can I use your laptop?" Ash asks Bri.

She slides it across the table to him.

"Pull up the email here," Ash tells me.

"What? Why?" I say, growing excited. "Can you trace it?" I log in to my email.

"I can probably find the general location it was sent from, which might be of some use."

Ash opens the email and clicks Show Original under the options menu, which takes him to a page that's a series of letters and numbers. He highlights the string of numbers next to Received and enters those into an IP search engine. A map location loads.

It's Mankato, Minnesota.

No way. My heart thumps against my ribs. "That's where Jen lived. So *she's* the one who sent the game to me? Why?" Anger flares in my chest. My life, my parents' lives, they're literally ruined—is it really because of some dumb gamer feud?

Ash thinks for a moment, his mouth scrunching to the side. "Well, demons are known to make deals, especially when their victim is desperate. I bet Jen didn't really have a choice."

"But why *me*? Why this anonymous email? It doesn't make sense. She could've just asked me to play it." I search for her name in my inbox. My breath catches in my throat. In early July, when I'd been unplugged following Riley's death, GinnySnow had emailed me six times.

They're all links to the game with a message from her that's a variation of "Hey, Viv, thought this would be a cool game for your channel!"

She really had sent it to me.

Ash reads the messages over my shoulder. "Maybe she got desperate when you didn't respond and started spamming it out to everyone she knew."

I slouch in my chair. "And I was dumb enough to play it." I massage my face. "She *knew* this was happening to me. That's why she apologized to me the day before she killed herself."

"Two months," Brianna interrupts. "Two months and six days. That's the time between when she first played and when she killed herself."

Two whole months? It's only been tormenting me for a little over a week—how much worse can things get?

"But what I don't get," Bri continues, "is if Ash is right and there was some 'demonic deal,'" she air quotes, "and Jen needed to get someone else to play the game, then wouldn't the demon have moved on from her—wouldn't that be the 'deal' part? Why kill herself now?"

Ash pauses, thinking.

"Maybe too much damage was already done," I say, my voice coming out a whisper. What if I didn't have Ash? What if no one believed me at all? I can see how Jen got to the point where taking her own life seemed like the only escape.

"Yeah," Ash says. "Maybe the demon succeeded and turned everyone against Jen. So even when it moved on, she was still alone."

Bri stares down at her notepad. "Damn."

I lean forward, wrapping my arms around my stomach. What am I going to do?

"If it really is all because of the game," Bri says, "we should try to find other people who've played. See if this has happened to anyone who's survived."

"I'm going to play it," Ash says. "The game itself could have some significance. Maybe there's something useful in it."

"No way," I respond. "I thought the same thing too, but it's too dangerous. And it's gone from my computer anyway."

"I'll download it on mine."

"No, don't!" I groan. "What if it starts mimicking you as well?!"

"Well, you said you told it a secret right? I won't. It's simple." He shrugs. "Don't worry," he continues, studying my face. "You can even supervise."

Bri didn't want to risk making herself a target too by playing the evil game, so she's staying home while Ash and I investigate *LOCKED IN*, which was a good call on Bri's part. How screwed would we be if all three of us ended up targeted by the demon? Ash and I huddle together at the computer in his room. His mom left half an hour ago for an overnight flight, and my mom thinks I'm staying at Bri's. My mom's too upset to even look at me right now, so she's given up on enforcing my grounding. Ash and I can play all night if needed. I still don't like this plan, but if Ash is right and something useful is in the game, we at least have to try.

Ash starts a new game of *LOCKED IN*. His character spawns in the long, dark hallway on the first floor of the abandoned apartment. The journal log opens, telling Ash that he's a reporter trapped in the building. He exits out of the menu and walks toward the staircase. The flashlight flickers, panning across the torn-up floral yellow wallpaper, dozens of cockroaches scurrying out of sight.

"What do you think we're looking for?" I ask.

"Not sure yet. How long did you play?"

"Not long. Got kind of bored after the third floor. It's hard to keep viewers engaged when the gameplay is just to unlock door after door."

"Then let's get to the areas you haven't explored yet." Ash's character approaches the staircase, but a thin gray barrier prevents him from going upward. A message pops up:

To ascend, you must complete the first floor.

I groan. "I hate these linear games."

"Just tell me what to do so we can get through it quickly."

I take Ash through all the same steps I did before: finding the clue in the jacket pocket, getting batteries out of the nightstand drawer. He enters the room where I'd told my secret the very first time I played, and it looks cheaply animated like it did when I streamed my second playthrough. The NPC is already here on the couch. A dialogue box opens.

What is the color of pain?

Ash types: vermillion.

He glances at me. "So, when you first played, this is where it asked you to tell it a secret?"

"Yeah, and the graphics of the NPC looked different too. Realer."

"Hmm. Maybe this is like the default version of the game, you know, demon-not-included mode."

The door behind the NPC unlocks, and we collect a key to

Apartment 31. An hour and a half later, after trudging through all the same gameplay I did before, we make it to the fourth floor.

"Uncharted territory, right?" Ash asks, pausing to take a drink of Diet Pepsi.

"Yep. Never went this far." I clutch my hands together. *Please, let something useful be here.*

Ash enters the first apartment on the right. The living room is startlingly cleaner than the previous ones we've visited: The walls are white with minimal wear. There's a sectional gray couch with a glass coffee table, almost like something out of Ikea.

"Weird. Why is the aesthetic so different?"

Ash shrugs. "Hopefully we'll find out." He enters the bedroom.

There's a modern white wardrobe and a desk with a slim computer. The closet is neatly stocked with brightly colored clothes. Ash searches the closet.

You find nothing.

The only thing amiss in the room—the dead, rotting woman on the bed, curled in a fetal position, blood staining her red hair. Ash clicks on the body. Nothing happens.

"This is why it wasn't a good game to stream," I say. "Way too much filler."

"Let's keep looking." Ash heads back into the hall, checking each apartment. They're all similar: modern and neat with a dead body on the bed or floor or couch.

I dig a chocolate brownie Fiber One bar out of my backpack and eat it, shaking my leg impatiently. When will we find something useful?

"Hungry?" Ash eyes my Fiber One bar. "I can order some real food. Pizza or something."

"Yeah, sounds good. But let's get this boring-ass floor over with." I throw the wrapper in the trash. I'm going to be pissed if we wasted hours in this game for nothing.

Ash enters the last apartment on this floor. The living room looks just like the others, furniture arranged slightly differently, like the programmer got lazier with setting design. Ash walks his character into the bedroom.

The walls are painted mint green. There's a pink ergonomic chair at a desk in front of a computer with a big monitor. Several anime posters hang on the walls. My pulse starts to climb.

"Look at the other side of the room," I say, my voice tight.

Ash pans the camera around.

A glass tank rests on the dresser, a white snake wrapped around a branch. The fleece throw on the mattress reads *Attack on Titan*. All the hairs on my arms stand up.

"Hmm, there isn't a body like all the others."

"Umm, Ash," I say, my voice trembling. "This is *my* room."

Ash hasn't been to my house, and I guess he hasn't paid close enough attention to my streams to realize that this room in the game is my room IRL. My hands shake as I pull up screenshots of me streaming.

"*See?!*" I hold the phone to his face and gesture at the game. "The chair, the color of the walls, the posters, my snake—Bakugo?! It's my room!"

Ash's eyes widen. "Oh shit. Freaky."

"What do you think this means?!"

He sits back, hands folding behind his head. "Well, all those other rooms had bodies in them, so like, maybe this is how the demon . . . archives its victims?" Ash's voice raises into an excited octave.

Oh shit. I put my hands to my head, heart pounding so hard I can feel it in my ears.

"Or maybe not," Ash says, noticing my panic.

I knew this thing wanted me dead. Ash's cousin said so, and really, what else could the demon's endgame be? But now, seeing my room in *LOCKED IN*, how it has those bodies in the other rooms—it's hitting me now that my death really is coming. It's not going to stop until it kills me.

"I don't want to die." My voice cracks.

"You're not going to die." Ash squeezes my hand, his tone serious again. "Let's keep looking. There has to be something here we can use against it."

I want to ask him what happens if we don't. What happens if we don't find a solution at all? But I stay quiet.

Ash continues from apartment to apartment. Some of the bedrooms look like they're from the '70s with orange retro patterned wallpaper. One apartment has a bedroom that looks like it's from the 1800s with an oil lamp, a wooden bassinet, and antique furniture. If Ash's theory's correct and the rooms are an archive of the demon's victims, then how do they date back so far if it finds them through the video game? This antique room was way before the internet was a thing people could even conceptualize.

"Do you think this bedroom is another victim room . . . or like part of the actual game?"

He gives me a confused look. "What do you mean?"

"Like, aren't all these rooms too old if the demon finds its victims through the game?"

Ash ponders that, scrunching his lips to the side while he thinks. I can't help but find the expression cute.

"What if the game is part of how it evolved to find victims? Demons are supposedly ancient, right? So I bet when this person was its target"—Ash gestures at the skeleton on the bed in the nineteenth-century-styled room—"it found them by, like, writing letters. It put an ad in the London paper or whatever. Now, it has the internet."

I groan. If Ash is right, then the demon is literally the virus from hell, and I handed it my identity and darkest secret on a silver platter. *Stupid, stupid, stupid.*

On the next floor, we try the first apartment, but it's locked. Apartment 31.

"Don't we have a key for this one?" I ask.

"Yeah." Ash opens the inventory and clicks Use Item.

The door unlocks. I lean forward. "Something good has to be in here."

Ash nods. His character enters the apartment. The walls are shredded and marred with bloody streaks, like someone had been trying to claw their way out. Ash walks into the bedroom, which is similarly derelict like the living room, except for the floor. It's covered in hair. Long, shiny, wet black hair. The strands wind up the bedposts and dresser, and they're slowly growing longer, snaking upward, engulfing the room.

"That's a really cool visual," I say. "Wish I'd found this room in my stream."

Ash side eyes me. "Uh-huh."

"Try that room." There's a door toward the back by the closet.

His character's movement is slowed as he walks over the hair, and I can't help but love that detail even though this game ruined my life. Ash opens the door. It's a bathroom, lit by a weak yellow light above the shattered sink mirror. Mouse carcasses litter the cracked tile floor. Cockroaches crawl out of the toilet bowl and up the walls. Ash's cursor passes over the shower curtain. A message prompts:

Pull open

Leave alone

Ash clicks **Pull open**.

The shower curtain moves to the side, revealing a tub full of blood and fleshy dark chunks. Flies buzz in the air.

"Cool."

Ash smiles, moving his cursor over the tub.

Feel inside

Go back

Ash clicks **Feel inside**. The speakers emit a wet squelching as his character rummages around. A message prompts:

Severed finger added to inventory.

"Alright." I glance at the clock: 10:19 p.m. "Three hours in, and we have no answers about saving my life, but we have a finger!" I roll my eyes and groan.

Ash pats my shoulder. "We're not done yet."

Two hours later, we make it to the game's top floor. The walls are cracked, bare concrete. Broken glass litters the torn carpet. Instead of eight units like every previous floor, this one only has one. A single door. It's red, but not from paint—it's the texture itself. Moist and dark red, like flesh.

I bite into another slice of the pizza we'd taken a brief break to order. "Get closer to that door," I tell Ash, my mouth full.

Ash's character walks toward it. The door glistens when the flashlight pans over. It *is* flesh. Wet, smooth muscle. The door moves slightly, like it's breathing.

"We have to go in there." My voice rises in excitement. Even though we're playing this game because I have a demon destroying my life, I can't help but feel that thrill from when I make progress in a tough game. This is the final level. We made it.

Ash clicks on the door.

Key required.

"Umm—" Ash starts.

"Use the finger!" I set the pizza slice down, leaning closer to the computer.

Ash hovers the cursor over the finger. It's bloodied, half of the dirty nail cracked off, the knuckle skin torn, revealing bone. He clicks **Use item**.

The finger floats from his inventory to the door, pressing into the flesh. The door undulates, swallowing the finger, and a hole forms in the flesh, big enough for his character to pass through. Ash walks forward.

I hold my breath. *This is it.* The big reveal.

He steps through, and the room is empty, the walls derelict and torn up, shredded.

"Try the corner—"

"Look," Ash says, cutting me off. "Those are names." He walks his character across the room and shines the flashlight on the torn-up wall. He's right, the walls aren't shredded, but carved. Hundreds of names are etched into the paint in uneven, jagged letters, like they were scratched in with someone's nails. Ash pans his flashlight across the room. Every wall, even the ceiling, is covered in names.

"What do you think they all mean?" I whisper.

"No idea."

"Look at that one." I point to the left corner. All the other names are simply etched into the concrete, but one name—*Looly Tuffin*—isn't carved, but written in blue ink, the penmanship clean cursive. "Why do you think this name is different?"

"Not sure, but we should write it down."

I type the name into my notes app.

Ash continues through the room, pausing so we can read the names on each wall. There are so many that the letters start to congeal together, but one last name catches my eye: Sweeney. First name: Jennifer.

A chill runs down my neck. "That's GinnySnow's full name. I mean, it's not the most uncommon name, so sure, it could be another Jen Sweeney, but . . . I feel like this one is her."

"Yeah, I don't think it's just a coincidence." Ash does the mouth-scrunching thing again.

"What are you thinking?"

"Maybe this room is a list of all the victim's names? A sort of trophy room? A manifest?"

I suck in a breath. "Umm, is my name here?"

"I haven't seen it, but we can keep looking."

Ash slowly shines the light in each corner and across the ceiling, and there—in the upper left side of the ceiling are the scratched letters: Vivia

"Oh shit. Do you think that's supposed to be my name"—my voice turns into a high-pitched squeak—"but it's, like, not finished?"

"Maybe—" Ash starts. The lighting in the game shifts, growing brighter. A shadow pans across the floor. Ash swings the camera toward the front of the room. A hole has formed in the fleshy red door.

It's getting bigger.

And bigger.

A clawed hand reaches through the hole. A cloaked head follows it, the eyes beady and orange. *Oh shit.*

The demon snakes through the door in one swift motion, the hole it entered slowly closing behind it. Ash's flashlight flickers out, leaving the screen black.

"Just shut off the game!" I grip Ash's arm.

Ash hits the Menu button. "It won't open." He clicks on it frantically.

Dark, long-nailed hands wrap around Ash's character's neck, the flesh mottled and scabby. The screen flashes red.

"Alt F4!" I yell. "Alt F4!" But Ash doesn't respond.

I turn to him. He's grasping at his neck, but nothing's there. What the fuck is happening? Ash's eyes bulge, his lips turning gray. Panic rises in my chest, my pulse pounding.

I put my hands on Ash's shoulders. "What's wrong?!"

His eyes roll back in his head.

I shriek and yank out the desktop's power cable, praying this will make it stop.

Ash bends down, coughing.

"Oh my god, are you okay?"

He wheezes. "Holy shit."

Tears sting my eyes. "Did that really just happen? Are you hurt?"

Ash sits up, massaging his reddening neck. "I'm fine." His voice is hoarse, his eyes red and watering.

I throw my arms around him, squeezing him tight. My racing heart begins to slow. If Ash had gotten hurt—or worse—I don't know what I'd do. The fear drains from my body, replaced with burning anger. "I told you not to play the game!" If Ash died, it would all be my fault. How could I live with myself if I got another person killed? "I never should've gotten you involved. I should just go." I start to move away, but Ash puts his hands on my back, pulling me closer to him.

"I'm okay," he says, his voice raspy and soft, speaking right into my ear. "I told you—I want to help. We're in this together. Besides, that was nothing." He chuckles and pulls back, smiling at me.

"If anything happens to you, I won't forgive myself."

Ash cups my face, wiping away the tear rolling down my cheek.

The gesture is so sweet, so comforting—if we weren't pretending to be into each other for the sake of my evil doppelgänger, I might think this is real. I might want it to be.

Bang!

A door slams shut from the living room, followed by creaky footsteps. My heart lurches. *Is the demon here? What do we do?* Ash and I lock eyes in wide panic.

"Ash! Flight got canceled," his mom yells. "I'm home!"

"Goddamn it." Ash stands, knocking the computer chair back. "Uh, get in there." He gestures for the closet. "Quick."

I dart inside, pushing myself behind his coats.

"What the hell, Ash?!" his mom shouts. "You didn't do any of the chores I asked you to?" Her footsteps approach his room. "I'm coming in." The door opens just as Ash slides the closet shut.

"What have you been doing all day?" his mom asks, her tone annoyed. "The dishes are piled up. I asked you to vacuum. You say you want a dog, but you can't even clean up after yourself?"

Aww, Ash wants a dog? I never pegged him for a dog person, but that's sweet. I smile, imagining Ash walking a cute little dachshund.

"*Yeah, yeah,* I'll get to it."

"Why is your neck all red?"

I cover my mouth. Oh no.

"It's called *autoerotic asphyxiation*, Mom. I told you to knock. Jeez, you do this to yourself."

Oh my god, what? Ash came up with the excuse so quickly, I wonder if he really has done that.

Ash's mom groans. "Seriously?" She pauses, probably taking in his room. Crap—where did I leave my backpack? I hold my breath. "I don't know what I even expect at this point," his mom continues. "I just wish you'd at least stop being a slob."

"Whatever. I'm going to bed."

The door slams shut. The light turns off. There's the sound of the fan turning on and the opening guitar riff of a Black Sabbath song. Ash pulls on the closet door, but it doesn't budge.

"It's stuck," he whispers through the crack. "Is it caught on something?"

"Umm." I glance down, lighting the area with my phone's screen. "No?" I try the door too, but it won't move. I feel for a lock, but there isn't one.

Behind me, something rustles, followed by the subtle screech of hangers sliding across the rack. Then a faint scratching sound. The scratching grows louder. Louder.

"Ash." My voice trembles. "Get me out of here." I pull on the door again, but it won't move.

"I'm trying."

I hold my phone with one hand and pry the door with the other, that awful scratching sound ringing in my ears. My phone falls from my hand, landing face down, so I'm in total darkness. I feel around on the floor and touch hair. Hundreds of strands of wet hair. What the fuck? I fumble for my phone, my fingers getting tangled in the hair. It starts winding up my wrists, tightening. I find the hard case of my phone and yank it out, tearing the hair away from my arms. I turn on the flashlight and hold it up, my hands trembling. The closet walls and ceiling are completely covered in slashes. They all say:

VIVIAN VIVIAN VIVIAN VIVIAN VIVIAN VIVIAN VIVIAN VIVIAN VIVIAN VIVIAN VIVIAN VIVIAN VIVIAN VIVIAN

"Let me out!" I push on the door, tears filling my eyes.

Ash's fingers pry between the door and the wall. I shove on it, using all my strength to break it open. The hair on the floor coils around my ankles, twisting upward around my legs, tightening like cords. I scream and pound my hands on the door.

"What the hell is going on in here?!" Ash's mom shouts.

Light fills the crack under the closet. The door slides open. My ankles are freed. I stumble out into Ash's room, sucking in shaky breaths. I turn behind me and the closet is normal. No scratches. No hair.

"Umm, *who* are you?" Ash's mom says, her voice accusatory. She has the same sandy-blond hair and striking eyebrows as Ash, and they're furrowed angrily at me. She looks at the closet, then at me shaking, then at Ash holding the door. Her expression shifts from anger to concern. "Ash, were you keeping this girl in your closet?"

"No!" he says. "She's uhh, she's just—"

"I'm his girlfriend." I steady my voice. "Sorry I was hiding in there. I didn't want to get him in trouble. I'll be leaving now." I pick up my backpack.

"You're Ash's *girlfriend*?" his mom says like it's unfathomable.

"Yeah." Oh god. What if she's really strict and anti-girlfriend and now he's in trouble? I hold my backpack at my chest, bracing myself for her to start yelling.

But instead of yelling, Ash's mom's face softens. Her thin lips curve into a smile. "You have a girlfriend?" She looks to Ash. "I never thought—" She pauses. "Never mind. It's too late to have girls over, but I'm glad. You're being a normal kid for once." She squeezes Ash's arm.

"Yeah, yeah, yeah." Ash's cheeks redden.

"Is that why your neck's all . . . ?" She gestures at the marks. "Are you two being safe? You know, it just takes one time and then you're pregnant, and your whole life—"

I experience my first full-body cringe.

"Nooo," Ash groans. "It's not like that."

"Uh-huh." Ash's mom takes a step closer to me. "I'm Linda." She shakes my hand.

"I'm Vivian."

"And you're so pretty too. Oh Ash." She beams at him. He looks like he might combust.

"Well, you be a gentleman and walk her out," Linda says to Ash. "And *ask* next time you want guests over." She winks at me and says more softly, "But you're welcome anytime." I thank her and wave goodbye, hurrying out the door.

"Sorry about that," Ash mumbles when we're outside. "So, what happened in the closet? The door felt like it had sealed shut."

I shudder. "More scary demon shit. I really need all of this to end before I lose it." The image of *Vivian Vivian Vivian* flashes in my mind, and my skin itches, like the hair is still slithering over me. I try to stop seeing those scratches, all that hair, but can't.

"I'm sorry I couldn't get you out sooner. I really tried—"

"I know. It's okay." I walk toward my car. "We never should've played the game—you almost got strangled to death!"

"I'm fine. 'Tis but a scratch." He gives me a reassuring smile. "And it was worth it. You remember that weird name? Looloo whatever?"

I glance at my phone. "Looly Tuffin." I forward it to the group chat with Bri and Ash.

"I promise I didn't almost die for nothing. That name—it has to mean something. And besides, you made my mom happy."

I blush, thinking of what she said about us being "safe." "She's nice. I thought she'd be pissed that I was hiding in your room."

"I did too, but I guess after everything . . . ehh. Never mind. You should get home." He opens my car door for me.

"No," I press. "After everything what?"

He looks down. "After everything that happened with my dad, she never thought I'd be a normal teen. She sort of just wrote me off as an antisocial freak." He shrugs. "I guess seeing you gave her hope."

"You're not a freak."

I pull Ash into a long hug, pressing my head against his chest. He squeezes me back. I tell myself it's because his mom or my demon could be watching and I need them to believe we're together, but really, I just want to hold him.

In the morning, I wake on the couch to the sound of the front door shutting. The living room feels ten times safer than my room, and I have actually managed to sleep for a couple hours. I sit up, blinking to adjust my eyes to the light. Dad's standing in the living room next to Mom. My chest swells with relief.

"You got released?" I stand and rush to him. "I was so worried about you."

His eyes are red-rimmed, his eyelids puffy. He's still wearing the same outfit they took him away in yesterday. I wrap my arms around him.

"I couldn't believe it when they arrested you." I bury my

face in Dad's chest, inhaling his familiar woody scent. "Why'd they change their minds?"

Dad doesn't hug me back. "They said you recanted, and without any physical evidence, plus the alibi that we weren't even here when"—he takes in a shaky breath—"when Riley passed, they didn't have enough to file criminal charges, so they released me."

I flinch, remembering that the doppelgänger had claimed that Dad killed Riley. That must've felt like I'd stabbed him in the back a thousand times over. "I'm so sorry this happened, Dad. I know it doesn't make sense, but I swear, it wasn't me. Soon, I'll have proof."

Mom stands beside Dad, looking at me with unexpected softness and pity. "We talked to Brian Clement, the grief counselor we met when Riley first passed." She dabs a tear starting to form in her eye. "Remember him?"

I nod. I remember how he smelled of patchouli and repeated the five stages of grief to us over and over. Where is she going with this?

"Well, we reached out to him again and he referred us to a child psychologist. We talked with the psychologist about you, about all that's happened this summer and your recent behavior." Mom clutches her hands together. "Honey, is there anything you want to tell us? Maybe we didn't talk enough about Riley."

"No! This has nothing to do with her. This is going to sound nuts, but you have to believe me." I inhale, composing myself. "There's someone who looks just like me ruining my life—a doppelgänger. She's the one who got Dad arrested."

Mom winces. Dad purses his lips.

Of course they don't believe me. "What about this child psychologist? What did they say?"

Mom puts a hand on my shoulder. "She thinks you might be acting out from the stress of Riley's death . . . as a way to cope and get our attention."

"*What?*"

"You used to tell all sorts of stories in middle school. Remember when we went to the Ozarks for a long weekend, and when we got back, you told everyone you'd been kidnapped? At your eleventh birthday, you told your friends that your father was a refugee from North Korea. Or the whole faked broken arm—"

"This isn't like that—this is *real*!" I told those stories so people would notice me. North Korean refugee was way more interesting than Japanese immigrant, and people already confused me with being half-Chinese or half-Korean all the time, so what did it even matter? How can my parents think that this compares to some dumb stuff I made up years ago?

Mom takes my hand. "Sweetie, we're trying to be patient because this is a compulsion. It's not necessarily your fault."

"I *literally* have an evil twin! It's out there right now, scheming ways to sabotage me, plotting—" I shut up, realizing that my words do make me sound like I'm making up a wild story.

Mom gives me a sympathetic smile. Dad frowns, his arms crossed.

"The child psychologist said we need to be patient and provide you with as much normalcy as possible right now," Mom continues. "We have an appointment for next Monday."

Dad walks away, like he can't stand to be near me.

"Am I still grounded?" I whisper to Mom.

"You can have your privileges back." Mom points a stern finger at me. "Within reason."

"Bri and I made up after that dumb fight we had." I never told Mom what it was really about, thankfully. "I think it'd help me if I can go see her, even stay the night this weekend?" I might be pushing it. Hell, I *know* I'm pushing it, but I need Ash and Bri's help.

Mom shifts uncomfortably.

"Mom, staying at Bri's is the most normal thing I could do. That's what the psychologist says I need. And Dad seems like he could use some space from me."

Mom sighs.

"I researched Looly Tuffin," Bri says, sitting next to me at the table at her place. "And guess what I found?"

"What?" I lean toward her laptop.

"She was committed to a psychiatric facility in 2003 in St. Louis and released in 2014. Reports say she attacked her boyfriend and claimed it wasn't her but her 'evil twin.'" Bri's eyes widen.

"Okay, what else?" I ask. "Is she around for us to talk to?"

"I found her on Facebook," Ash says, sitting across from us. "Posting weird alien conspiracy theories and cat memes. I messaged her."

"Did she reply? Will she call us? Or hop on FaceTime?"

"Umm," Ash starts. "It was kind of hard to get her to reply." Ash holds his phone up, showing me the messages. Looly has no profile picture, just the gray and white default avatar.

Hi Looly, Ash wrote, I'm a senior at Merton High in Iowa and am writing an article for the school newspaper about wrongful convictions. I read your statements from your arrest in 2003 and considering the way the media handled your case, my fellow classmates and I believe your story would be perfect for our paper. We'd love to interview you and get to know the truth. Are you free for a phone call sometime?

"I came up with the school article story," Bri chimes in. "Figured it would be better to approach her with something milder than 'how did you get rid of an evil doppelgänger that tried to sabotage your life?'"

I give Bri an appreciative nod.

Ash shows me the several follow-ups he sent:

Please, Looly. We need to write this paper to pass and it's too late to change topics now.

We need you.

Your cat is really cute.

She responded to that last one:

Ok. But no more internet communication. Not even Facebook is safe. Can meet at Starbucks in Hemlock, Missouri. The one on the corner of Fields street. Will sit at counter.

"Hemlock, Missouri? I've never even heard of it, but St. Louis is pretty far." I type the town name into my maps app. "Nine *freaking* hours." Ugh.

Bri groans. "Even if we were to go, when could she meet?"

"Tomorrow." Ash scrolls down, showing us Looly's last message.

Free tomorrow at 10a.m. Logging off now.

I glance at the clock. 4:00 p.m. If we leave now, we can make it with time to get some sleep and be ready to meet Looly in the morning. I stand, grabbing my backpack.

"Oh, hell no," Bri says, "that demon has been in your car, your house, Ash's closet. You really want to drive nine hours to meet a stranger?"

"I don't have any other leads. If we leave right now, we can get there tonight." I pick up my keys.

Ash stands, smiling slightly. I love that he's always down for an adventure.

Bri throws her arms up. "This Looly person might not even have any useful information at all. I really don't like this. . . ."

I clutch my hands together. "I have to at least try. Please, Bri? And you're the only one who's eighteen. You can get us a room."

Bri lets out an exasperated sigh.

I press my hands together. "I really need your help with this. Besides, I thought you loved road trips?"

"Yeah, to *Disney World*, not on a wild goose chase to Missouri. I don't know, Viv."

"I'll owe you forever and ever. Whatever you want—" I rack my brain for something I can offer, but really, Bri's the one who already has the nicer things. "I'll do anything! I'll do your laundry for a month and clean your car, and, and—"

"*Fine*," Bri says, one hand on her hip. "But we're taking your car, I get control of the music the whole way, and if you get to have an overnight adventure with your boyfriend, then I'm bringing Eric. We should stay on the buddy-system anyway, all things considered."

"Yeah, totally fair." I haven't talked to Eric since the whole sext debacle, so this will be awkward, but the more people around me, the safer I'll feel. "How much does Eric know about my evil twin situation?"

"Basically, none. He's not really one to believe in any of what you've got going on." She gestures at me and Ash like we're a chaotic mess. "So let's just rope him in on a need-to-know basis?"

"Sounds good. What about your parents? Will they notice we've disappeared?" I glance toward Bri's mom's office, where she's buried in paperwork.

"They'll be busy with meetings and the corporate merger

my mom's working on. Besides, I'll tell them we're going up to the lake house for a study marathon."

"Great." I glance at my phone. "I think I should leave my phone at the lake house in case my mom checks my location." I hate hate hate the idea of doing that, but Mom will definitely be checking my location, especially since she thinks I'm lying about everything, which isn't entirely untrue. The lake house has spotty connection, so it's a perfect excuse as to why I can't answer when she inevitably texts to check in.

We pile into my car and pick up Eric, who also dupes his parents with the "study marathon" lie. Then we swing half an hour out of the way to drop my phone off in the lake house mailbox and get on the road to Missouri.

I stare out the car window, watching the corn whipping by as we cross the Iowa state border. I don't know if it's the gas station pizza upsetting my stomach or just cold feet over this plan, but three hours into the trip, all I want to do is puke. Would it be better to get out of the car and disappear? *Can* I run away from the doppelgänger, or would it be able to find me wherever I go?

"You okay?" Ash asks, leaning closer to me in the back seat.

In front of us, Eric's driving, Bri scrolling on her phone in the passenger seat. I keep my voice down so Eric doesn't overhear. "Do you think if this plan doesn't work, I should just run away? Change my name and move?"

Ash frowns. "I'm sure the doppelgänger has a way to find you, like it can sense where you are or something."

"Oh, so you two do talk?" Eric says, not with a douchey vibe but in his genuine, chatty himbo way.

"Yeah, we do," I deadpan. I'm not in the mood for small talk.

"With how quiet and solemn you two are, you'd think we're going to a funeral." Eric chuckles.

"Leave them alone," Bri says. "They're emo."

"We should tell him the password," Ash whispers to me. "In case the doppelgänger tries to trick him again."

I nod. "Eric, I need you to remember something. A word. It's important."

"What is it?"

"Vermillion."

"Is this a road game or something?"

"No, it's serious."

"What's it for?"

"Just remember it, *okay*?"

"Vermillion? Hmm. Isn't that a city in *Pokémon*?" He laughs. "I like this game! Okay—your turn. What game is the city Bruma from?"

Thirty rounds of naming what video game the city Eric's thinking of is from (which I win) and four Beyoncé albums later, we arrive at our destination, stiff from the car ride and tongues raw from Sour Patch Kids. I park the car in front of the Airbnb

Bri rented: a small brown two-story duplex near a strip mall. It was my turn to drive the last three hours, and all I want to do is lie on the floor and stretch my back.

Bri punches the pin into a lockbox, retrieving a key and unlocking the building door. We walk upstairs into our unit, stepping onto the old, creaky wooden floor. In the living room, there's a floral couch, a leather recliner, and a small flat-screen TV. A hallway leads to a room with a queen-sized bed.

"Not bad for fifty dollars," Bri says. "So, you two are good in the living room, yeah?"

I feel like it would be safer if we all slept in the same room, but I don't want to make it weird for Eric. "Yeah, that's fine."

Bri pulls Eric by the hand into the bedroom. "Night, lovebirds." They disappear into the room before I can come up with a quippy retort.

"Sooo . . . you want the couch? I'll take the recliner." Ash gestures at the La-Z-Boy.

"That works."

I sit on the couch while Ash tucks himself into the recliner, pulling a fleece blanket around his shoulders. He scrolls through his phone, and a few minutes later, he's passed out, snoring softly.

I'm too jittery from the caffeine I had on the drive to fall asleep. I move from the couch to the floor, lying on my back and pulling my right knee across my chest. My back releases with a satisfying pop. Much better.

In the bathroom, I brush my teeth and change into sweats, then lie on the couch. Normally, I spend half an hour reading video game subreddits to help me fall asleep. Without my phone, I don't know what to do to help me wind down.

I flip from my back to my side, sweat forming on my brow and back. It's hot AF in here and the blanket around my feet is scratchy. A smoke detector chirps from the kitchen.

Beep.

Beep.

Beep.

I can't take it anymore. I sit up, my stomach grumbling. I haven't had any real food since Taco Bell a few hours ago.

"Ash," I whisper. "Are you awake?"

No response, then a loud, drawn-out snore.

Muffled chatter comes from Eric and Bri's bedroom. I walk toward the door, hand raised to knock, but pause when I hear Eric say Ash's name.

"Why is Viv hanging out with him now?" Eric says. "I thought she was the one who voted him the 'school shooter'?"

My stomach churns. I feel like such an ass for having ever said that.

"Well," Bri starts, slowly choosing her next words, "it's complicated. He's been helping her out with something, and he's not that bad. He's actually kind of smart."

"Huh."

I smile at Bri's words. To hear someone like her, who's popular in a conventional way and not just in a niche way like me, say something nice about Ash might mean a lot to him. I'll have to tell him when he's up.

I knock on the door.

"Yeah?" Bri says.

I open the door. "You want to grab something to eat? There's a McDonald's on the corner."

"I could use a snack. Coming?" She nudges Eric.

Eric's playing on his Switch, his lower half tucked under the blankets. "Nah," he says, eyes still on the screen. "Bring me back a couple cheeseburgers?"

Bri and I slip on our shoes and go outside. "It's right there." I gesture at the McDonald's down the street. "Let's just walk?"

"Def. I feel like the Tin Man from being in the car so long." Bri bends down, stretching.

"It's nice getting to hang out again," I tell her. "I've missed you."

"Same. Those few days we weren't talking, I was sad. Like real sad."

"Really? You seemed fine when I saw you at school."

"I was *pretending* to be fine."

That makes me feel a little better. I wipe my sweaty brow. I thought the humidity was bad back home, but it might be even worse in Missouri, like walking through warm, wet gauze.

"Thanks for coming. Not just to McDonald's, I mean the whole trip. I know it's not what you had planned for this weekend."

"It seems safer to stay in the loop in person. This whole thing is so scary and wild. Besides, Eric and I have never gone on a trip together."

"Have things been weird since the whole fake sext thing?"

"At first, yeah. But he knows it wasn't really you, and we're good now." We stop in front of McDonald's. Bri looks me in the eyes. "I haven't gotten to say this in person yet—I'm really sorry for how I acted then. I called you a slut." She cringes. "And that was not okay. I *hate* that word. And then I ignored you like a total raging bitch in the cafeteria. I don't know what I was thinking, I mean, I wasn't. And the whole time you were actually in danger, and I didn't believe you. I'm so sorry."

"It's okay."

She makes a pained expression.

"Really." I give her a reassuring smile. I push the McDonald's door open and walk in, holding it for Bri. "But I appreciate the apology." It feels good to have my best friend believe me.

Bri and I order our food and two burgers to go for Eric, and I get one for Ash, just in case he's hungry too. We sit in a booth to eat. My hand reflexively goes for my pocket so I can check Twitch, but of course, it's not there. *Ugh.* I walk to the counter to get more ketchup. Something moves through the window in the parking lot, crawling low on the ground, scuttering under a car.

A raccoon? Except it seemed bigger. A shiver trails down my back, my hairs standing on end. And then I see it: me, staring back through the glass. My doppelgänger.

My heart rate skyrockets. A small scream escapes my lips, ketchup packets falling from my hands. I stagger backward and the doppelgänger does too. *Wait.* I run a hand across my head and so does the reflection. No winking. No creepy smile that's not mine.

It's just a reflection.

"What's going on?" Bri shouts, standing at the table, her eyes wide.

"It's okay!" I let out a relieved chuckle and pick up my ketchup. An older white woman at the soda machine throws me an annoyed look. I return to Bri. "Just got freaked out by my own reflection. It's cool."

"Girl," she presses her hand to her chest, "you gave me a heart attack."

When we get back to the Airbnb, the building door is locked.

"Aww shit," Bri says, searching her pockets. "The door must've auto locked. And I don't have the key." She pulls out her phone and starts calling Eric.

I take a few steps back onto the lawn, where I can see the living room window. In case Eric doesn't pick up, I'll throw a rock to get Ash's attention.

"Ugh, he's not picking up," Bri says. "He's probably deep in *Pokémon*. Do you have Ash's number memorized?"

"No. Is there a rock somewhere?" I take a couple more steps back. The living room is dark, but I can make out the silhouettes of two people chatting. Perfect. Ash is up and he's talking to Eric.

"Found one." Bri holds a small rock in her palm.

"Never mind. They're in the living room." I start waving my arms. What could Eric and Ash possibly be talking about? I jump up and down to get their attention.

The living room light turns on. My stomach plummets.

Eric is not shorter than Ash, and he definitely does not have boobs and greenish-gray hair. Oh fuck.

"Not me!" I yell, flailing my arms. The doppelgänger steps closer to Ash, putting a hand on his shoulder.

I shout, "DOPPELGÄNGER!" but Ash can't hear me.

Bri lets out a high-pitched panicked scream. "Holy shit, it looks just like you!" She clutches her phone. "Should I call the cops?"

"What are they going to do?!"

"I don't know!" Bri cries.

Bri and I watch as the doppelgänger plays with a lock of her hair, smiling at Ash. There's no way he's going to fall for this. But what will the doppelgänger do when she realizes Ash knows what she really is?

Ash puts his hand up, gesturing at the scar on his palm from where we'd cut ourselves. I glance at my palm. The cut has mostly healed now, but the mark is still visible, the skin red and tender. The doppelgänger lifts her hand too and I can't tell from here, but the way she's confidently showing off her palm, I'm 99 percent sure she has the mark too.

Vermillion! I shout internally.

Bri throws the small rock at the window. It bounces off the glass with a *clink*. "I don't know what I thought that would do!"

The doppelgänger's head jerks in our direction. She sees us. Oh shit. While she's distracted, Ash punches her in the face. I almost wince seeing my own nose crumple in like that. The doppelgänger staggers backward, flickering to black for a moment like she's glitching out. Does that mean she *can* be hurt?

The doppelgänger smiles and reaches in her pocket, then flips open a knife. *Shit, shit, shit.* I jump up and down screaming, "RUN, Ash!" The doppelgänger lunges at him with the knife, but Ash slides to the side so quickly, it's like he just did an IRL dodge from *Assassin's Creed.* "Now, hurry!"

Ash darts past the doppelgänger and for the door, but then he stops.

What is he doing?

The doppelgänger's mouth moves. She's saying something to Ash.

His head turns slowly around. He holds eye contact with the doppelgänger, listening to her. His mouth twists in . . . disgust? Pain? The lights turn off, and I can't see anything.

"Ash!" I scream, pulling on the front door handle.

Thirty seconds pass. Then a minute. What is happening? What if the doppelgänger is hurting him? Killing him?

A moment later, Ash opens the front door.

I rush across the lawn, hugging him. "Oh my god! Are you okay?"

"I'm fine." He pulls away from me, his tone unusually glum. "Vermillion, so you know it's really me."

"What happened? What did the doppelgänger say? Is she still in there?"

"We should go check on Eric," Ash says to Bri, ignoring me.

"Ash—"

He turns and goes back upstairs.

Ash and Bri run up the stairs. I follow them. We stop at our unit's door and nudge it open. The living room is clear. I reach into my backpack, grabbing the iron knife.

"Ash, what did the doppelgänger say?"

He doesn't answer me.

I swallow. Whatever it was, it was bad enough to make him clam up. Maybe something about his dad . . . or something about me? My heart rate kicks up.

A cough comes from the bathroom. The toilet flushes. Bri and I glance at each other, then we tiptoe down the hall. Ash puts his hand on the doorknob. I raise the dagger, ready to stab the demon in the head. Ash whips the door open.

I lunge in, aiming for the demon's head with the blade. But the demon doesn't look like me—it looks like Eric.

"What the hell?!" Eric backs up as I shift my weight to avoid stabbing him, but the dagger is heavy and the sudden change in my trajectory makes me ram it into the wall, scraping away a long slash of paint. The dagger clatters to the floor.

"What are you doing?!" Eric takes out his AirPods. "You know these places have outrageous damage fees?"

"Shit, sorry! It's not so bad," I say, thumbing the damaged wall. *Wait.* I still don't know where the doppelgänger is—I don't know that this really is Eric.

Ash steps into the bathroom. "Password." He raises his own knife at Eric.

"*What?*"

"The word Viv asked you to remember!" Bri pleads with him. "It starts with V—"

"Don't help him!" I throw her a look.

"Oh *right*," Eric says. "Vermillion City."

I exhale. Ash lowers his knife.

"Sorry about that." I pick up my dagger.

"Why are you all freaking out? What's with that weird knife?" Eric eyes the serpent engraving on the dagger. "Did you really just try to stab me?"

"No—"

Bri squeezes my arm. "I think we really just need to tell him what's going on."

"Okay." I sigh. She's right. Keeping him out of the loop is only more dangerous. "You know how you got those messages and that picture of 'me,' but I told Bri it wasn't really me?"

"Yeah . . ." Eric raises an eyebrow. "I thought that was all fake. Someone hacked your accounts."

"Not someone, but some *thing*. Look, this is going to sound crazy, but I have an evil doppelgänger that's hellbent on ruining my life." My eyes start to shine with tears. "It's trying to turn everyone against me."

Eric is silent.

"I know it sounds wild, babe." Bri takes a step closer. "But it's true."

Eric looks between me and Bri, lips pursed. He bursts into a laugh. "This is totally a horror LARP, isn't it? Are you streaming this?" He looks around me for a hidden camera.

I groan. "We're not role-playing!"

"*Suuure*." Eric holds his hands up. "I'll play along." He walks into the living room. "Where's the food?"

Bri gives me an exasperated look. "Maybe we should just leave it at that."

"Probably. And we need to search the place," I say, already checking the shadowed corners. "Make sure the doppelgänger isn't still here." If Eric wants to make a game out of it, then whatever.

I look under the bed and in the closet while Bri and Eric search the living room and kitchen, Eric whining that he's hungry. Ash sits on the couch with his arms crossed. The doppelgänger is gone. For now.

Bri takes Eric's hand. "Let's grab the food, babe." They

head down to the lawn, where we'd dropped the McDonald's in our panic.

I turn to Ash. "What happened? What did the doppelgänger say?"

He looks to the side, his jaw locked. "That *you* were the one who started the rumor that I was most likely to be the 'school shooter.'" His voice hitches. "That you were the one who told people I collect dead opossums."

My blood flushes cold. "I didn't—" The urge to lie and deny kicks in instinctually. But I did say those things, didn't I?

Ash scoffs. "It said you would deny it, but that there's proof on your Instagram, from last September. So, I checked on my way downstairs. And sure enough, you posted that quiz you made. You know that rumor went through school and the principal called me to his office because he was worried I was actually a school shooter? After he searched my backpack, he called my *mom* and lectured her about all the signs of a school shooter. She's spent the last year fretting that I'm going to end up in prison like my dad."

My stomach falls. I never thought anything like that would actually happen. I totally forgot about that reel. "It was a joke, Ash. I'm sorry. I barely even remember that—"

"Exactly." His teeth clench. "That's how insignificant I am to you."

I flinch. "That's not what I mean—"

He scoffs. "You probably think I'm an idiot for helping you all this time. Like I'm just your little plaything following you around—"

"I don't think that! I'm sorry, really. I said stupid stuff, but I didn't mean any of it. It was a dumb, bitchy thing that I did."

Ash's face softens a little, but he doesn't say anything else.

"Will you still come with me to meet Looly tomorrow?"

He's quiet. If Ash bails on me now, I don't know what I'll do. "I can't do this alone, please, Ash. I need you. I'm so sorry I said those awful things about you."

I take a step closer, and he recoils, sinking farther into the couch.

"I'll go with you tomorrow," he mumbles, still not looking at me.

Bri and Eric return, holding the crumpled McDonald's bag. Eric's already a few bites into his first burger. "Vermillion!" Eric says, mouth half-full. "I should say it every time I leave and come back, yeah?"

"Yeah," I say. "That's not a bad idea."

"There's an extra." Eric pulls another burger out of the bag. "I got it for Ash."

"I'm not hungry," Ash says, his tone frigid.

I look down. There's a moment of tense silence.

"Umm, who died?" Eric asks. Bri slaps his arm. Eric shrugs.

"For safety," I look around the living room, "we should all sleep together in here. And one of us needs to keep watch."

Bri nods.

"Wow." Eric starts unwrapping the burger meant for Ash. "You guys are really serious about this LARP."

I groan. "Yeah, whatever."

"I'll keep the first watch," Ash offers, his tone still chilly.

"Okay," I say. "Wake me up in two hours?"

Ash gives a small nod, then he and Eric carry the mattress from the bedroom to the living room. Ash sits on the couch while Eric and Bri lie on the bed. It's too narrow for me to sleep next to Bri so I curl up by her feet like a cat. I keep trying to make eye contact with Ash, but he sits turned toward the window, one arm draped over the couch, his eyes focused on something outside.

At 10:00 a.m., Ash and I walk in awkward silence to the Starbucks where we agreed to meet Looly. Eric wanted to have a date with Bri instead of tagging along to interview a stranger for our fake school newspaper, which he also thinks is related to our "LARP," so they're having brunch at the diner across the street. And Eric might still be a little freaked out that I tried to stab him.

The Starbucks is packed, but I still spot Looly immediately—it must be her because she's the only person who looks like they're on the verge of a nervous breakdown. She's a frail white woman, blue eyes bulging behind thick glasses, knees shaking, sweat stains streaking the sides of her purple shirt. Her features are dainty, her fine chin-length hair a very light blond.

"Her message said she'd meet us at the counter," Ash says.

"Pretty sure that's her." I smile and wave at the skittish woman at the counter.

Looly gives an unsure wave back. She stands, eyes darting around, clutching her big yellow purse like she might run out of here.

"Hi." I approach her cautiously, a warm smile on my face. "Looly, right?"

She nods. "Hello."

"I'm Vivian. This is Ash."

Looly chuckles nervously. "I thought you'd be older. Are you really here for a journal?"

"We're seventeen." I smile. "It's a school journal."

Looly glances to the corners of the room, muttering incoherently under her breath, her mouth moving quickly, teeth nibbling her lip.

"Yeah, so . . ." I continue. "We were hoping we could interview you about your experiences with, you know, the 'evil twin.'" I air quote. "But we totally believe you by the way. We want to give a voice to the wrongly imprisoned."

"It wasn't me," Looly says. "I need everyone to know that. It *wasn't* me."

"We know, that's why we wanted to meet. So, what more specifics can you tell us—"

"It's not safe to talk about here." Looly's eyes lock onto mine, their bright blueness intense. Her eyes dart around again, and I follow their gaze. She seems to be looking at the security cameras and laptops on the tables.

"I thought you wanted to meet here?" Ash asks.

"To see that you were real." Looly pinches Ash's arm skin, gently tugging at it like she's testing its human pliancy. Ash flinches but doesn't stop her. Looly lets go of his arm.

"We're real," I say softly to Looly. "We're just high schoolers." I reach my hand out for her to touch. She gives my hand a firm pinch and jiggle. I'm glad Bri's at brunch with Eric—she would *not* like this.

"So . . ." Ash says calmly, "if Starbucks isn't safe, then where is?"

Looly nibbles on her pinky nail, mumbling. "Never know when it's watching . . . never know who it might be." She looks around, then pulls a baseball cap from her bag and puts it on her head, tugging the brim down. "Only my home is safe."

I glance at Ash, not entirely sure I want to follow this grabby Facebook stranger back to her house, wherever that may be, but what if her place is actually safe from the doppelgänger? What if she has information that can help me? We didn't drive all the way here for nothing.

"Is it far?" I ask.

"Far?" Looly says. "Yes. Has to be. Off the grid."

"Okay. Like how far is far?"

"An hour? Maybe closer to two? Depends on road conditions," Looly says toward the floor.

Ugh. Bri wanted the car so she and Eric could go to the city if we were going to be long. Welp, sorry, girl. "Okay, we'll follow you. I just need to get my car." I turn to Ash. "I'm going to grab the keys from Bri. Hang out with Looly for a second?" This woman looks like she might bolt any second, and I can't let her bail on us now.

"Yeah," Ash says, his voice still monotone.

I wince, wishing he would just talk to me like normal again.

I dart across the street and into the diner, where Bri and Eric are sharing a platter of pancakes.

"I need the car keys," I say to Bri.

Eric groans. "But we were planning to go to the city to check out the mall. They're going extinct."

"Sorry, but I really need the car." I turn to Bri. "I have to follow Looly to her place 'off the grid.'"

"*What?*" Bri pauses, fork halfway to her mouth.

"Yeah, it sucks, but I need this. I'm sure you guys can find something fun to do around here."

Eric snorts. "Yeah, right."

"And it might give me time to talk to Ash because he totally hates me now."

"Why?" Bri continues eating.

"He knows I made that quiz saying he was most likely to be school shooter."

Bri's eyes widen as she takes the keys from her purse. I snatch them from her.

"Look, maybe you can help me with damage control on this? Say something nice about me to Ash? Help make him forgive me?"

Bri frowns. "It hurts when you lie to people, Viv. Especially your friends."

"Yeah." I look down. "You're right." I lied to Bri once, years ago when I said I couldn't go to her thirteenth birthday party because my mom was in the hospital. Really, I was jealous of Bri's fancy party, and I didn't want to watch her open all her nice presents. I didn't think my mom would run into her mom at Target that weekend. Bri didn't talk to me for a week, and I swore I'd never lie to her again.

"If you're really sorry," Bri continues, "you have to tell him yourself."

I nod. "I will." I've kept my promise to Bri: I haven't lied to her since her thirteenth birthday. Except about Riley, but that's different.

That's a lie I have to keep telling not just her, but everyone.

Ash and I get into my car, following Looly's rusty old truck to "off the grid" land. Ash sits with his arms crossed, his head turned away from me.

"So, do you just hate me now or what?" I ask.

Silence.

"Please say something."

After another minute, Ash speaks. "I thought we were genuinely becoming friends, and now I feel like you're just using me."

"We ARE friends!" I shout. "Genuinely. Look, you want to know the truth? I do stupid, mean things online for attention, okay? I'm an insecure, attention-seeking bitch—there, I said it.

My content isn't even original. I saw a girl on Twitch make a quiz ranking all her classmates and I thought it would be a good idea. I didn't even think about how that quiz would hurt you when I made it; I just thought about how it would get lots of views and make my classmates notice my channel, and saying it out loud now"—my voice cracks—"yeah, I realize that's really fucked up. I'm sorry."

We stop at a red light. Ash's arms uncross. "You could've told me sooner. We should have full honesty, so there are no weak points for the doppelgänger to exploit. If there are lies between us, it's only going to use that to make us turn on each other."

I nod. "You're right." I look away from the road to meet his eyes. "I really am sorry."

"Just promise that you'll be honest with me from now on?"

"Yeah, I will." I turn my head back to the road. He's right. But I can't tell him the truth about Riley. I just can't. It's unforgivable.

We merge onto the freeway behind Looly, and a few minutes later, she takes an exit so last second, I fear she's trying to ditch us. I glance over my shoulder and swerve the car to stay on her tail. We follow Looly a few more miles down a winding road, then she turns onto a dirt path with dense tree coverage overhead.

The lack of civilization and Looly's *Jeepers Creepers*' truck reminds me of the opening act of a horror movie, and Ash and I are the stupid teens wandering right in to be massacred. How do I know Looly isn't a serial killer? Or even the demon in a new getup? I don't. And that's how desperate I am for help.

Looly's truck plows through the off-road terrain, smoothly rolling over dirt and rocks. My little car struggles to keep up, but I keep my foot down on the pedal. *Please, don't get stuck. Please, please, please.*

A few sketchy miles later, Looly's truck abruptly brakes in the road. I slow to a stop behind her.

"What do you think she's doing?" Ash asks, and the tightness in my chest softens. He's talking to me again, and his tone is normal.

I look around for Looly's house, but there's nothing out here. Just a lot of trees.

Looly gets out of the truck, holding a rope and bucket. *Oh shit.* "Umm, Ash?"

"Maybe . . . it's a bathroom thing?"

"Phones!" Looly approaches our car, jiggling the bucket. "Laptops."

"What?" I roll down the window.

"No phones. Laptops, tablets, Fitbits—none of that past this point. No electronics." She holds the bucket up to the window.

"Uh, okay," I respond, trying to sound polite. "May I ask . . . why?"

"Will explain when it's safe," Looly whispers.

Ash leans over me, dropping his phone into the bucket. He

opens the backpack at his feet, pulling out both my laptop and his.

"I don't have my phone."

Looly's eyes narrow at me.

"Really, my parents took it."

"You're sure this is all?" Looly pushes her head in, big eyes darting around.

"That's all," Ash says.

Looly ties the rope around the bucket and throws it onto a branch, pulleying our electronics up into the air.

"Umm, is that necessary?" I ask.

"Yes." Looly ties the rope around the base of the tree.

"And if it rains?" I follow up.

Looly doesn't answer me.

We continue along the road for another half hour. Looly's truck rolls to a stop in front of a gray trailer home. I park behind her, stretching my back as I step out of the car. Weeds are overgrown at the bottom of the trailer home. The front door is secured with several locks. Looly inserts a key into each lock, turning them one at a time. Ash stands beside me, slapping mosquitos off his arms.

Looly undoes the last lock, then looks around before finally pulling the door open.

We follow her inside and I gasp, quickly turning it into a fake yawn. The windows are covered with aluminum foil. Wooden crosses hang on every open space on the walls. There's an antique wood stove that's the kind of thing I would build in a survival game.

"I love your place, Looly."

Looly doesn't respond and shuts the door behind us, sending the whole room into complete darkness. The only sound is Looly securing each latch on the door.

I fumble around for a light switch, but I can't find anything, only foil and crosses.

"Got any light in here?" Ash asks.

"No. Completely off the grid," Looly answers.

"Cool," I say. "Very ecofriendly."

We stand in the dark for another awkward thirty seconds, and I can't help but think again that Looly might be a serial killer. Visions of our bloodied bodies in the bathtub spin through my mind, a podcast host describing how Ash and I were found dismembered in a trailer. Finally, a light flickers on. Looly stands in front of us, holding a battery-powered lamp.

"If you're off the grid, then how did we get a hold of you through Facebook?" Ash asks, a hint of suspicion in his voice. "Just curious."

Looly sits at the table, gesturing for us to join her. "I use the public library for my outside contact. Gets lonely around here." She places the lamp on the table. "So, what do you want to know for your paper?" A gray tabby cat leaps from a shelf onto Looly's lap. She pets the cat behind its ears, Looly's tense shoulders easing.

"We want to get a full profile of you, so tell us a bit about your background." I pull a notebook and pen from my backpack. "Where you grew up, what your family was like, your hobbies as a kid."

Looly starts talking about how she grew up in Arkansas, the middle child of a librarian and plumber, how her passion as a kid was ice-skating, and her words flow out of her mouth in calm, complete sentences, not the skittish Looly we've seen so far. Hopefully, now that we've buttered her up, she'll spill the demon beans.

"Amazing," I say. "So, shifting gears into your wrongful conviction, the articles we read stated that you had a mental breakdown and attacked your partner in a 'manic state.' Can you tell us more about that?"

"I didn't have a mental breakdown, because the person who attacked Travis wasn't me," Looly says, massaging behind the cat's ears. "But someone who looked like me. A twin. An evil twin."

"But you weren't born with this twin, right?" I ask.

Looly shakes her head.

"How'd it start for you?" I lean closer to her. "How did the twin find you?"

Looly's eyes narrow at me. "How do you know it 'found me'? Why don't you believe the news article?"

I fidget. If Looly gets freaked and doesn't want to talk anymore, this whole thing will be for nothing. "Well, it's just too wild of a claim, you know? We figured there must be some truth to it. And if you did have an evil twin, I figured it must've started at some notable point in time."

Looly sits back, shoulders easing. "In 2002, I had a gambling problem. Put my family in debt. My fiancé—he lost our house because of me." She fidgets with the table cloth. "I joined an anonymous online support group. Told them about my problems, the lies I told to get money. The horrible things I did." She shudders. "The guilt."

"Is that why you don't allow electronics here?" Ash asks. "Because you think the online support group is how it found you?"

"I know that's how it found me. *It* came to me at night," Looly says, pronouncing 'it' with grave emphasis. "Through the computer."

Looly rolls up her sleeve and studies a mark on her arm, a patch of white scars beneath her elbow crease, the same circular pattern as mine.

"How'd you get that?" I ask.

"It stood beside my bed, sunk its nails into my flesh."

My hand goes to the mark on my arm. "Did you have sleep paralysis?"

Looly tenses. "I never told anyone about that." Her eyes narrow at me.

Shit. "Oh, you sure about that?" I stall. "Because I swear—"

"Show me your arm," Looly orders.

I inch back. "What? Why?" I chuckle nervously.

Looly's nails dig into the table. The cat leaps off her, running away. "Roll up your sleeve," Looly hisses through gritted teeth.

I roll up the sleeve of my good arm, showing her my clear skin.

"The other one," Looly snaps.

"We're just students," Ash says. "Really, Viv doesn't even know what you're talking about."

I nod. "Yeah, I don't—"

Looly lunges forward, yanking my sleeve up. Her eyes widen, expression twisting when she sees the scabs on my arm.

"GET OUT!" She stands over me.

I stand too. "Wait, Looly. I need help. *Please.*"

Looly pauses, holding her hands to her face. "It feeds on you. You're cursed. Doomed." She continues muttering to herself.

Behind Looly, there's a family photo on the wall. In the center is a teen Looly with round, rosy cheeks and a big smile. She's holding a state championship soccer trophy, her parents standing beside her, beaming. If it weren't for the same tiny nose and pointy chin, I wouldn't recognize that girl as this woman in front of me. Looly was normal once. And the demon did this to her. I cannot end up hiding off the grid for the rest of my life. I just can't. She needs to tell me how to make it stop, right now. "How did you get it to leave you alone?" I plead. "How do we kill it?!"

"Kill it?" Looly laughs. "It's not alive to begin with. It's an undying evil, and it feeds on your pain, your guilt." Looly backs away from me toward the bedroom. "It only moves on when it takes what it wants."

I move closer, clutching my hands together. "What does it want?"

"*Everything.*"

"Can you be more specific, please?"

"Your sanity, your pain." Looly whimpers. "Your life." She covers her face with her hands. "It left me with nothing. Now get out before it follows you here!" She opens a cabinet to her right and begins rummaging around. "*Go, now!*"

I have no idea what she's searching for, but it wouldn't surprise me if it was a gun.

"Let's go." Ash grabs my hand. I head outside with him and turn back to see Looly standing in the doorway, holding a shotgun.

"One more thing." Looly's intense blue eyes lock on mine. "Don't take the deal."

"What deal?"

She slams the door shut, the locks clicking into place.

Great. What was even the point of all that? My hands clench into fists. "I can't believe I triggered her with the demon scar." I groan. "How was I so stupid?"

Ash opens the passenger car door. "I think that's all we were going to get out of her anyway."

"Yeah. A whole lot of nothing."

After wasting an hour searching for the tree where Looly hung our electronics, then picking up Eric and Bri from the Hemlock Museum of Natural History, we make it back to Merton, Iowa at 11:22 p.m. Two hours and twenty-two minutes past my curfew. Mom and Dad are going to be pissed, but at this point it all seems hopeless anyway. What does it matter if I'm grounded if my whole life is screwed? Looly's words echo in my mind: *You're cursed. Doomed.* Food for the undying evil.

I already felt SOL before meeting Looly, but now that the one doppelgänger survivor has diagnosed me as officially unsavable, it feels ten times worse.

I open the mailbox at Bri's lake house, retrieving my phone. 10 percent battery and eleven missed calls from Mom. I close my eyes for a moment, the guilt for making her worry gnawing at me.

I text Mom back: im alive. Just got service back. Phone about to die. Home soon.

At least now she won't think I'm dead in a ditch somewhere.

"Everything okay?" Bri asks when I get back in the car.

"*Totally*. Parents hate me. Demon's going to kill me. I'm exhausted. It's a blast," I say, oozing sarcasm.

"Sorry, jeez," Bri mumbles, folding her arms. In the back seat, Eric wraps an arm around her and frowns at me.

We stop at Eric's place first. "Sorry the LARP didn't go how you'd hoped," he says, stepping out of the car.

I close my eyes. "Thanks, Eric."

He bends down, giving Bri a kiss. She half-heartedly accepts it, still pouting.

I feel bad about my shit attitude, but it's really hard to take all this in stride. I turn up the radio, not speaking for the rest of the drive. When I pull up to Bri's house, she gets out of the car quickly, slamming the door behind her.

"Hold on." I step out.

She turns back to look at me, her face saying *Now what?*

I wrap my arms around her. "I'm sorry for being snappy. I really appreciate you and all your help."

Bri softens and squeezes me back. "I know you're stressed.

We'll figure something out. Text me when you're home."

I return to the car and start driving Ash to his apartment, my grip tight around the steering wheel.

"How are you feeling?" Ash asks.

"Like I should just run away." I pull up to his place, parking beneath a streetlight. I shut the car off, closing my eyes and leaning back against the headrest. "And keep running and running."

"I'd come with."

"I'm being serious."

"Me too."

I glance at him. "Even after that quiz? And all the things I said about you?"

He shrugs. "I'm getting over it. It's not like you're the only one who's said something like that about me."

I know he isn't really getting over it, not deep down inside, and he shouldn't be. "I really am sorry." I take his hand. Pretending to be Ash's girlfriend, spending time with him—it's the best thing that's come of this whole shit show. And if I'm being honest with myself: I am into him. The fact he's believed me since day one—that alone has catapulted him out of the friend zone, and he's not even close to being the creepy loser I'd assumed he was before all this. He's a good guy. "And I like you, a lot."

Ash's cheeks turn pink. "I've always liked you, Viv. Ever since freshman year when Ms. Klein made us give an artistic presentation on *Of Mice and Men*, and you did that truly bizarre interpretive dance with the bunny ears and ribbons around your wrists."

My face heats. I thought it was so cool and original at the time but then people started making memes of my dance. I was so humiliated I blocked the memory. "You remember that?"

"It's seared into my brain. You were all I thought about for the rest of the year."

My chest bubbles with warmth. "Seriously? You never talked to me."

"I did, actually. Or tried to at least, but you brushed me off."

I cock my head to the side. I have no memories of Ash talking to me. Was I that obsessed with myself, I never even noticed him?

Ash reads the concern on my face. "It's okay. You were busy, and I didn't try hard enough, I guess. Figured you were too cool and mainstream for me anyway." He takes his hand from mine, unbuckling his seat belt. "Call me when you get home, so I know everything's okay?"

I don't answer because I'm consumed by a radical thought: *I should kiss Ash.*

I'm not the type of girl to kiss first. I haven't even thought about wanting to kiss a boy since all the Tristan drama. But I should take risks, should do the things I want, free from fear of embarrassment or rejection. And I was wrong about Bri having the only decent guy at our school. Ash is right here in front of me.

I lean across the console, fumbling to unbuckle my seat belt. I was hoping to do this smooth and quick, but it's obvious I'm coming in for a kiss, and Ash isn't pulling away. Instead, he seems to be waiting for this, welcoming it. My lips meet his and his hand cups the back of my neck, his lips parting to kiss me back. His lips are soft but his mouth tastes smokey, and if we're going to be a real thing, I'm absolutely making him quit the cigarettes. His tongue brushes against mine and I stop noticing the smokiness, my body consumed by a warm, tingling thrill.

Ash and I kiss for another minute, hands holding each other's necks like we may never get to kiss again. I reluctantly pull back, glancing at the clock.

"I really should go," I say.

"Let's run away," Ash blurts, his face glowing. "For real. We'll live off the grid, no electronics, like Looly. Then the doppelgänger can't find us. And we'll keep moving, just to be safe."

I don't want a life on the run, and how could it even be practical? "But what about school? What about money?" *What about my Twitch dreams?* I don't say that out loud. At this point, even I'm starting to accept that I can't focus on my Twitch career with the doppelgänger ruining my life.

"School's a scam. I never planned on going to college anyway. And money—I have a bit saved up from my theater job."

"What about my parents? Your mom?"

"If they knew what you were going through, they'd understand. My mom will be okay."

"But what about—"

Ash takes my hands. "What other options are there? If we can't kill it, we have to run."

I don't want to admit it, but maybe he is right. "Let me think about it, okay? I really have to get home."

"Right. You sure you'll be okay tonight?"

No. "Yeah, don't worry."

"Vivian Mei Sakamoto-Reynolds—where the hell have you been?" Mom stands in the kitchen, one hand on her hip and the other balled in a fist on the counter.

"I told you, we went to the lake house, Mom." I drop my backpack on the floor, fatigue overcoming me. I can't even remember the last time I had a decent night of sleep.

"Why didn't you answer any of my calls?" Mom's eyes narrow at me. "And don't say 'bad signal'—my texts were delivered. You could've driven to get a signal and called back."

"Ugh. I don't know. I'm sorry!" I look to Dad, who's sitting at the kitchen table quietly.

"Kenji," Mom says. "Why don't you tell our daughter what's going on with work? Hmm? Then she might have something to really be sorry about."

"What do you mean?" I ask, my pulse spiking. "What's going on?"

Dad massages his brow. "The people of Merton aren't exactly keen on using my services after my arrest."

My stomach drops.

"You need to understand that your actions and words have consequences, Vivian," Mom says.

I nod, the urge to cry building in my chest. "I'm sorry. I'll find a way to fix this, I promise." I spin on my heels and run upstairs to my room. I yank open the closet door to grab my sweatpants and freeze, my blood running cold—it's not my closet in front of me, but a long dusty, decrepit hallway that ends in a staircase. The walls are covered in yellow floral wallpaper marred with scratches, the floor littered with rodent carcasses, cockroaches scurrying up and down the walls.

Oh hell no.

The light behind me flickers off. I step back and my foot slides on something soft. I glance down, squinting in the darkness. Riley's *Frozen* dress, wet and bundled on the floor. My heart leaps. I turn to run for my bed, but there's only more of the same dark hallway. A faint light glows from several yards away at the very end. My bedroom.

"Vivi," a little girl's voice calls from the staircase behind me. "I want to show you something."

I cover my mouth, my chest aching. The voice sounds just like hers.

"Vivi, don't you want to see me?"

I run for the light at the end of the hallway, the voice still calling for me. *It's not Riley. It's not her.* Tears blind my vision and my foot catches on the shredded carpet. I stumble and reach to balance myself on the wall. Something sharp scrapes the palm of my hand—a broken fingernail. Dozens are embedded in the shredded wallpaper, jagged and bloodied. I shriek and keep running for my room, but with each step, the floor beneath me lengthens, my bedroom inching farther away.

"*Look at me, Vivi!*" the voice behind me calls, growing closer, angrier.

I sprint as fast as I can, fueled with adrenaline, and burst into the light of my room.

"Leave me the fuck alone!" I scream at the closet, slamming the door shut.

I lie on my bed, pulling my knees to my chest, sobbing. A hard lump forms in my throat. I sit up, trying to breathe, but something's blocking my airway. My chest heaves with the urge to gag. I open my mouth to cough up whatever I'm choking on but can't produce any air. My lungs ache. I stand, clawing at my throat, panic searing my veins. I whack myself in the chest to knock the thing blocking my airway loose. Something shoots out of my mouth. I double over, sucking in air. I wipe my eyes and kneel to see what the hell I was choking on.

In the middle of the floor, coated in saliva, is a quarter-sized brown button.

"Vivian?" Ms. Newman says. "Can you hear me?"

"Huh?" I sit up straighter at my desk, snapping out of a sleepy haze. These last few days, I've been wearing the same clothes, too afraid to open my closet, slogging my way through life in a paranoid, depressed haze, constantly looking over my shoulder. Whenever I see my reflection in the mirror or on the camera of my phone, I blink eight times and pinch my pointer finger and thumb together to make sure it's really me.

Ms. Newman approaches my desk, brows furrowed. "Can you stay after class?"

"Sure." Clearly, I'm failing, which sucks because I'd always looked forward to taking Dystopian Lit, but due to recent circumstances IDGAF anymore. At this point, running away might be my only option. My next Twitch paycheck comes on Friday, and even though it'll only be enough to maybe cover a tank of gas, I need every penny I can get to fund my nomad life.

I spend the last ten minutes of class rubbing the button in my pocket. I had the instinct to throw it away, burn it, pitch it into the lake. But I deserve to constantly be reminded of what I did.

When class dismisses, I approach Ms. Newman at her desk. She peers at me behind her glasses, her blue eyes full of warmth and concern. "Is something going on at home?"

I shake my head. A cockroach scurries up the wall behind Ms. Newman, disappearing behind the clock.

"Your outline was due last week. I haven't received anything from you."

"Yeah . . ." Three more cockroaches crawl out from behind the bookshelf. That's too many cockroaches, right? Am I seeing *LOCKED IN* everywhere now? Am I going Looly-level insane? The thought makes me want to sob-laugh. Is there even a point in running away if the demon is literally in my mind?

Ms. Newman continues talking about what I should do to make up for my missed assignments. I nod politely, watching the bugs behind her.

"You have such lovely skin," Ms. Newman says.

My eyes flash to her. "*What?*"

"Hmm?" Ms. Newman looks up from her desk. "I said you could go." She stands to walk me to the door. Another cockroach scurries across the floor.

Ms. Newman quickly stomps on it, smearing it off her shoe. "Damn things are everywhere."

After school, I stand at my bathroom sink, brushing my teeth. Something itches and rubs against my eyelid. I set the toothbrush down, pulling the skin around my eye open. An eyelash floats on my sclera. I try to flick it off with my nail, but the eyelash drifts around the corner of my eye. Annoying, but whatever.

The rubbing sensation in my eye comes back. Ugh. I turn back to the mirror, pulling my lower lid down again. Three eyelashes are floating in the whites of my eye. I scrape them out, but then another drifts out from beneath my eyeball and onto the pink flesh of my inner lid. I flick it out. Another wriggles out from under my eye, crawling like a worm. *What the hell?* I blink furiously, splashing water into my eyes.

The other eye starts to itch too. I look up at the mirror, but my vision is obscured, lines blocking my view. I lean closer. Dozens of tiny black hairs crawl over my eyes. They keep coming until darkness consumes my vision. I feel for my eyes and scream when I touch only prickly hair.

I wake to the sensation of my chest being crushed. My eyes

flash open—they're not covered in hair. *It was just a dream.* Relief washes over me. I try to roll onto my side, but I'm immobilized, my limbs tense and frozen at my side. *Shit, okay, you're still dreaming, just wake up. Wake up.*

"I'm here to make an offer," a quiet feminine voice whispers in my ear. "A deal."

I try to speak, but my lips are still sealed together. Saliva pools in my mouth. *Shit.* I'm going to suffocate. Drown in my own drool if I can't move.

The voice chuckles. "I'll give you some air to think about it."

The weight releases from my chest, and I suck in a breath. Crouched at the edge of my bed is me. My heart skips. I've seen the doppelgänger before, but never this close, never right in my face. Once the shock wears down a little, all the hatred for this bitch comes flooding in. I lunge for her.

"Ah, ah, ah." Her freezing hand wraps around my throat. Her grip is inhumanly strong, like a metal vice. "You get one chance to accept my offer."

"What is it?" I say through gritted teeth.

"You get someone else to play my game." She trails a finger along my cheek. "Someone with secrets." The nail turns from my chewed stubby one to a long, hooked claw. "And all this goes away. I'll even give you a parting gift. Send you subscribers in droves." The voice shifts from feminine to deep and guttural. "*That is what you want, right?*" the demon says. "*Fans? Validation?*"

The low, rumbling tone sends goosebumps across my skin. "*Money to help your parents?*"

I swallow. Could the answer to all my problems be this easy? But could I really do this to someone else?

"*What more could you want?*"

"What I want is for you to leave me, my friends, and my family the fuck alone."

"*I will,*" she says, still speaking in that awful, guttural voice. "*You just have to do one thing.*" She smiles, the brown of my eyes flickering to orange.

What if I just blasted links to the game on the internet? Got some stranger to play? I wouldn't even have to know who would suffer from this. But could I live with myself knowing I ruined someone else's life? But what about my life—my parents' lives? Don't I deserve happiness again?

"*I can bring you more subscribers than you could ever dream of,*" the demon says. "*The choice is so simple.*"

I think of GinnySnow, the decision she made. *Don't take the deal*, Looly had said. Could I really do this to someone else? Haven't I ruined enough lives already? Is it even worth it? Jen took the deal, and the demon still ruined her life anyway.

"No."

"*Are you sure? You don't want to do anything you'll regret.*"

"Fuck you. I'm not going to do this to anyone else."

"*That's what they all think,*" the demon says, letting out a low chuckle. "*At first. But you'll change your mind.*"

My breath catches in my lungs. Is it going to do something even worse than before? "Don't hurt anyone else," I plead. "You can keep tormenting me, but leave my friends and family alone."

The doppelgänger smiles. "*Stupid, naive girl.*" Her clawed hand covers my face, pushing me back onto the bed. "*Sleep.*"

My head meets the pillow and I plummet into another nightmare.

THREE MONTHS AGO

I yanked Riley out of the tub, cradling her in my arms. "Rye!" I tapped her cheek. What happened? Had she fallen in? "Come on, wake up." She didn't respond. Her eyes were glassy and half-open. *Oh no. No no no no no.*

I set her on the bathroom floor and pressed on her chest, tilted her chin back and blew air down her throat, all the steps I could vaguely remember for CPR, my hands numb and shaking so badly I could hardly control them. I tried CPR again. Again and again and again. Riley's head lolled to the side, her chest remaining still, completely unresponsive. Her hazel eyes stared blankly at the ceiling. Panic struck me like lightning.

Oh my fucking god she's dead.

But people could be saved after they'd drowned, right? She couldn't be dead. I held my ear to her chest, listening for a pulse, but couldn't hear over the sound of my own heart pounding. I blew air into her mouth again, noticing now how her lips were so cold and purplish. *No.* I blew more air into her mouth, pressed harder on her chest. *Come on, breathe.*

I reached for my phone to call for help, but I'd left it in my room, and a dread of horrible certainty was slowly creeping over me: I was too late. Riley was beyond resuscitation.

I scooped her up and held her. How had I let this happen? Had she struggled and called for me? Why did I have to be wearing a headset? The thought of her yelling my name felt like a knife carving through my stomach. Why did I leave the tub full? Why didn't I stay with her like I was supposed to? I held Riley to my chest, rocking back and forth. The panic slowly left my veins, replaced with insurmountable despair and self-loathing.

How was I going to tell Mom and Dad? How could they stand me after I'd killed Riley? I couldn't even stand myself. I looked at the tub, envisioning drowning myself too, but I was too cowardly to go through with that. There was no way I could tell Mom and Dad I'd let this happen. I curled up on the floor with Riley, her wet *Frozen* dress soaking my clothes and the rug beneath us.

What if . . . what if I could make it seem less like my fault? My self-loathing tripled—I'd just killed Riley, and still I was thinking about me me me. I wailed into Riley's wet hair.

For a while we lay like that, me praying for her to *wake up, please wake up.* I pulled my knees to my chest, and then I felt it in my pocket. Mom's button. "Toddlers can choke on just about anything," she'd said when child-proofing the house. "We should really find that button."

I held the button up to the light, studying this small, innocuous object, a heinous idea unfolding in my mind. Drowning was like choking, wasn't it? I shook my head. There was no way I could go through with this plan.

But I was already a bad person. Terrible, really. So what did it matter at this point? What would be worse for Mom and Dad: knowing I'd let Riley drown in the tub while I was on Twitch, or letting them think she'd choked on something? What if they could believe this was an accident that could've happened even while they were here?

What if I could make this look like it wasn't my fault?

I wake to a series of texts from Bri.

i'm still thinking about what you said last night

i could barely sleep after that

why didn't you tell me sooner?

I bolt upright. What is she talking about? I try to remember what Bri could be referencing, but can't think of anything. This reeks of doppelgänger.

I text her back: can we meet in person?

Brianna: yah, where?

Me: i'll come over?

Brianna: my parents have friends here

I think of the most public safe place. Looly seemed to think the demon moves through electronics somehow.

Me: whitecreek park, by the jungle gym in 20 min?

Brianna: ok!

I park near the creek and walk toward the jungle gym. It's a hot, sunny day. Not too humid. The type of day when Riley was alive where I would go on a short jog to assuage my guilt for sitting so much, then stream for six hours straight. I turn the bend of the path, jungle gym in sight. There's Bri, sitting on a swing.

When I get to her, her eyes are puffy like she's been crying. She stands and hugs me. "You could've told me sooner."

"Umm . . . told you what?"

She wipes her nose. "How Riley really died."

My stomach drops, my blood chilling. "What? She choked on a button—"

Bri's face twists, realization crossing her face. "Holy fuck." Her eyes widen and she takes a step back. "It wasn't you, was it? But you said Vermillion."

How did it learn our password? I said it on the phone once, didn't I? So stupid.

"I should've known," Bri continues. "Goddamn it."

"What did it say?" I hold my breath, fear gripping me. *Did it tell Bri what I did?*

"You called me last night. I was suspicious at first, but you sounded so emotional, and you said you had to tell me what really happened to Riley." Bri puts her hands to her head. "I don't know why I thought it was real. Because it felt so honest?"

I look away, tears stinging my eyes. This cannot be happening.

"And you just tried to lie to me again." Bri's voice rises. "Tell me the truth now, for real. How did Riley die?"

"She—" I start, my throat constricting. *She choked.* That's all I want to say. *It wasn't my fault—she choked.* But Bri already knows. "She drowned."

Bri wipes her eyes. "And I had to hear the truth from your goddamn doppelgänger. I thought I was your best friend, Viv."

"You are!"

Bri lets out a pained laugh. "Last night, I thought you were finally telling me something real. But the realest thing I ever heard from you wasn't even actually from you. You're so fake, Viv."

"Bri, I—"

She turns away. "I can't deal with this." She walks quickly down the path. I want to go after her, but what can I even say?

I sit on the swing, my head down. I wipe my nose on my sleeve. Bri hates me. What am I going to do? There's nothing I can do to fix this. If I'd just told her the truth in the first place, would things be okay between us? No. Even if I'd told her the truth back when it happened, she would've hated me then too. And she *should* hate me for what I did, for lying about it. For everything. I lean forward, crying into my lap.

A scream echoes through the trees, shrill and panicked.

My head shoots up.

There's another scream, followed by people shouting.

What the hell? I jump up and run on the trail toward the noise.

A few joggers and a couple bikers are gathered around the gazebo. A slow trail of blood snakes down the pavement. My breathing quickens, my hands growing clammy. Please, don't let something bad have happened to Bri.

"Someone call 911!" a woman cries.

"Is she breathing?"

I push through the crowd. *Oh fuck, no.* Bri is sprawled on the ground, blood spewing down her forehead, her white tank crimson. Her arms are gashed open, split and exposed. The flesh is so red, so red. Like raw steak. People aren't supposed to look like this.

I fall to my knees beside her. How could this happen to Bri? She was so careful and smart. She was trying to stay out of my mess, and this still happened to her.

"Bri, can you hear me?" I reach to touch her but pull back, not wanting to hurt her. Her eyes roll back in her head. I turn to the crowd, standing there on their phones. "Is an ambulance on the way? Can somebody help her?!"

"Hey!" a man yells. "She's the one who did this!"

I turn back to see who they're talking about.

A man in a silver bicycle helmet points at me. "I saw her. She came out of those trees"—he gestures toward the right—"and stabbed her!"

"Yeah!" someone else yells. "She changed clothes, but it was definitely her! Look at her hair!"

I shake my head, words impossible to form. Blood is still flowing freely from Bri's arm and stomach, the crimson pool around us growing. She's unconscious, so it shouldn't hurt if I touch her, and I'm supposed to put pressure on the wounds, right? I try to remember any first aid advice I've read but my mind is full of panicked static. I open my backpack, unwrapping the shirt around the serpent-engraved knife. I secure the fabric around Bri's arm. It soaks through, but I clamp down on it. *Stop the bleeding, stop the bleeding.*

Sirens blare nearby. "They're almost here, Bri. Hold on."

"Get her away!" a woman yells.

Hands are on me, pulling me back from Bri.

"Stop!" I yell. "I'm trying to help her! She's my best friend!"

A man holds my right arm and a woman my left. I thrash against them, trying to get back to Bri, but they only clamp down on me harder.

"Over here!" the woman yells, waving to someone with her free hand. "We have her!"

Cops jog toward us. I don't even care if they're going to arrest me, I just need them to save Bri. Paramedics follow the police, thank god. *Please, please save her*, I silently chant.

An officer takes my arm. "I have her now," she says. A bystander holds up her phone, filming me. The paramedics lay Bri's limp body onto a gurney. My stomach knots, vomit gurgling in my throat. I swallow it down.

Another police officer approaches me. I recognize him. Officer Jones, who arrested Dad, the one I tried to show the footage of my doppelgänger. His eyes narrow at me. "You again," he snarls, then says something else, but I'm too focused on Bri. The EMTs load her into the ambulance, shutting the doors.

"So, what happened?" Officer Jones says, snapping his fingers in front of my face. "Your friend piss you off?"

"What?" I croak.

"What'd the poor girl do? Steal your boyfriend or something?" He shakes his head in disgust. Cold hard metal clamps around my wrists. The woman officer starts reciting my Miranda rights.

The vomit comes for real this time. I spew green bile onto the sidewalk and a little on my shoes, my throat on fire.

"Get in," Officer Jones says unconcerned. He nudges me onto the plastic back seat of the police car and shuts the door.

I sit in the back of the police car, my legs sticking to the seat, sweat pooling beneath me. My mind spirals down a dark, shitty drain.

What if Bri dies?

Is this all my fault?

Yes, yes, yes.

"I said let's go!" the officer barks.

I blink a few times, my vision refocusing. Officer Jones stands beside me, his gut at my eye level, holding the car door open. I hadn't even noticed we'd arrived at the station.

"Okay, yeah." I get out of the car, my whole body shaking. Once I'm standing on asphalt, my legs almost collapse under me.

"This way," the officer says impatiently, gesturing with his right hand and holding my backpack in the left.

I don't move. If I step forward, my legs will fold in half. He sighs impatiently and grips the back of my shirt, steering me toward the brick building. We step through the station's glass doors, the air conditioning a shock to my sweaty, bloody skin. The officer leads me to a desk where an older white woman with silver curly hair sits behind a transparent protective barrier.

The officer undoes my handcuffs. I massage my wrists, the skin tender from where the metal had pressed in. But how can I even think that this hurts when Bri was literally butchered? *What if they put her on morphine and she gets addicted and her whole life is ruined from here on out? What if she can't go to college next year? What if she's already dead?* My mouth salivates like I'm going to puke again, but my stomach doesn't have anything to spew up.

The silver-haired woman slides a plastic bag through the slot under the protective barrier. "Put your things in here," she says with a Southern twang.

All I have in my pockets are my phone and a hair tie. I place them in the bag. The officer sets my backpack on the counter.

"That everything?" he asks me.

I nod.

"You need to call your parents." Officer Jones gestures to the landline on the wall. My stomach backflips. I've been so worried about Bri that I haven't even thought about how Mom and Dad will react to all this. *Shit.* I pick up the phone.

I press 2-8-8 for Mom's number, then pause. What's the rest of her number again? I knew her number by heart in elementary school, but now? No idea. "Umm, I need my phone. Need to look up my mom's number."

Officer Jones snickers. The silver-haired woman blinks at me like I'm a moron, then unzips my phone from the bag, sliding it with a judgmental push across the desk.

"No funny business," the officer says.

Like I would really be able to do anything that constitutes "funny business" with my phone in five seconds. I scroll to Mom's number and punch it into the landline, then hand my cell phone back to the secretary.

"Hello?" Mom says.

"Hey, Mom. It's me."

"Hi, Viv." Her voice shifts to concern. "Where are you calling from?"

"The station," I say. "Uh, the police one. Bri was attacked—can you come down here?"

"*What?* Are you okay?"

"I'm fine."

"Viv, I don't understand," Mom says, her voice climbing to a high, strained tone. "What happened—"

"I have to go." I hang up, not able to stand the fear in her voice. I stuff my trembling hands in my pockets.

The officer leads me to a bare room and shuts the door, leaving me alone. I sit on a plastic chair, scraping the dried blood out from under my fingernails. Visions of Bri's maimed corpse flash through my mind. No. *Not* "corpse." She's alive. She has to be.

Fifteen minutes later, the officer opens the door again. Mom and Dad stand next to him, their faces pale and grave. Mom's gray T-shirt is inside out. She must've been in pajamas and thrown on clothes so quickly, she didn't realize her shirt was on wrong. She's always so well put together; she wouldn't make a mistake like that unless she was truly hysterical.

"Please, take a seat." Officer Jones gestures to the chairs next to me.

Officer Jones sits across from us, looking at his scrawled notes on a yellow legal pad. "Witnesses claim that Vivian was on the trail at Whitecreek Park, where she was seen stabbing Brianna Davis at 9:07 a.m. She suffered eleven stab wounds."

Mom covers her mouth. "People saw *Vivian* do this? No. She would never."

Dad stiffens. "No, no way."

"It wasn't me," I say, but my voice comes out a faint croak. I repeat again, louder this time: "It wasn't me."

"Oh really?" The officer's eyes narrow. "Then why do we have half a dozen witnesses claiming they saw you?"

"It was someone who looks like me."

"Then why did we find a knife in your backpack?"

Shit. Claiming "that's my demon knife!" will get me a one-way ticket to an asylum. "It's for self-defense. Test it for blood—that's not the knife that was used!"

"Oh, we will."

Good. Maybe that will get me out of this mess. But how long will that take?

"What happens next?" Dad asks the officer.

"Your daughter is facing assault charges. Considering that she's seventeen, she could be tried as an adult." Officer Jones glares at me. "You better hope that the victim pulls through, or you could be on the hook for murder."

I gulp, staring down at my hands. If Bri dies . . . I can't even think like that right now.

"Vivian wouldn't do this," Mom says. "Bri's her best friend. Viv's not violent—"

Dad puts a hand on her arm. "Cheryl, we need to look at the facts. Vivian hasn't been herself lately."

My stomach backflips. Dad really thinks I did this.

Mom cries, holding her face for a long moment. "This wasn't Vivian's fault. She wasn't in her right mind." And Mom thinks I did too.

"It wasn't me!" I shout, exasperated.

The officer's eyes narrow at Mom and Dad. "I'm sure the prosecutor will factor her mental health issues into the sentencing, but you should've kept her on a shorter leash."

Are Mom and Dad going to be held responsible for this too? Guilt coils through my intestines. I can practically feel the ulcers growing inside me. I bend over, gripping my head. Mom, Dad, and the officer continue speaking, but their voices and the room are blurred.

Mom touches my back. "Viv, we're taking you home."

"I can leave?"

The officer nods. "We don't have enough to charge you—yet. So, you can go home, but we expect you to *stay* home." He gives Mom and Dad a serious long stare.

But *should* I go home? What if my parents are next on the doppelgänger's kill list? Might they be safer if I'm locked up? They will be if the doppelgänger doesn't want to expose itself since no one's going to believe that I escaped jail. "Are you sure?" I ask Mom. "Everyone could be safer if I stayed in jail."

The officer brightens, seeming to like this idea. "As much as I appreciate you acknowledging the severity of your crime, you're not in charge of that decision."

"Oh sweetheart." Mom hugs me. "We would never let you stay in jail."

"Can I see Bri?" The words leave my mouth without me thinking them through, but I need to see her. I need to know she's okay.

The officer scoffs.

"Please. Let me see her." I turn to Mom and Dad.

"Not happening," Dad says. "You're going straight home."

I walk quickly to the car. As long as I'm the doppelgänger's target, no one in my life is safe. It's probably planning some way to kill Ash or my parents right now. I get in the back seat of Mom's car, staring out the window at the cloudy sky. Riley used to love sitting on my lap outside the house on the grass, looking at the sky and babbling that the clouds were "sky pillows." Guilt snakes through my intestines.

Riley died because of me.

Bri is in the hospital because of me.

This whole thing started because I killed Riley. It really is all my fault. I can't keep living like this. I can't stand the fucking guilt anymore.

Dad gets into the driver's seat. Mom buckles her seat belt beside him, quietly sniffling.

I lean forward, squeezing each of their hands. "Mom, Dad, I'm really sorry for all of this, and I just need you to know—I love you."

"We love you too," Mom says, though her voice is small. Dad doesn't respond at all.

I lean back in my seat. There's only one way to stop the doppelgänger, only one way to end everyone's suffering.

I'm going to give it what it wants.

I sit in my pink gaming chair and text Ash: I'm going on Twitch. I have some things to say. You're going to hate me after this, but I have to tell the truth. Please tell me you'll watch

Ash: ok, what are you talking about

Me: just watch. You'll understand

I open my drawer, placing the facedown picture of me and Riley on her first Christmas on the desk. My vision blurs as tears stream down my face. I'm so tired of holding in all the guilt, so tired of telling all these lies.

I log in to Twitch and title the stream "Confession and Goodbye," and I go live.

Viewers start logging in.

what game is this?

what's wrong?

omg are you crying?

what do you mean goodbye viv??

"Guys, this is my last stream. I've had an awesome time gaming with you, and I'm so thankful for all of you, but I'm done. I can't do it anymore."

why????

noooooo we luv you

good ur overrated

you're my fave!!! don't go!!!

im here, Viv

I look at the username of that last comment. It's Ash. *I can do this.* It's like I'm just talking to Ash. "But before I quit Twitch, there is something I have to confess. You might remember that I took a long break this summer because there was a tragedy in my family. My baby sister died."

omg yeah what an awful accident

so sad

Ash: Bri is logging in too. she's awake

My heart skips. Bri's awake. *She's alive.*

"Well, I lied to you. I lied to everyone, my parents, my best friend." I suck in a big breath. *This is it.* The words I've thought a million times but haven't been able to say out loud. I'm finally going to do it. Not only will Ash and all my Twitch fans hate me, but I'm going to be canceled, socially ostracized, disowned by my parents. But after I do this, I can finally be free from some of this guilt, and the next time the doppelgänger shows up to kill me, I'll probably just let her. "It wasn't just an accident—" My voice cracks. A stabbing ache pierces my chest, the words a lump in my throat, but I have to say them.

"It was my fault. I killed her."

I did it. The words actually left my mouth, and they rolled off my tongue easier than I thought they would. Probably because this is Twitch—my element—not in person, and more than that: I just don't fucking care anymore. I'm ready for everyone to hate me. I'm ready for my life to be over. As long as it means no one else has to hurt but me, the demon can win.

Chat messages flow in, but I can't stomach what they might say, and my eyes are too blurry to read anyway. "My parents were out of town—they went to Chicago to see a play. I was supposed to be watching Riley, but I started streaming while she was in her room."

I wipe my eyes and go into detail about the worst day of my life.

THREE MONTHS AGO

A robotic numbness overtook me as I went through the motions of removing Riley's soaked *Frozen* dress and drying her off. *I'm doing this to protect Mom and Dad*, I told myself. *This will make it easier for them.*

But I knew I was doing it to protect myself, to go without blame, to still be loved by them. I drained the tub and took Riley to her bedroom, where I redressed her in dry clothes, pulling her limp arms through the sleeves of a shirt. Then I opened her lips and pushed the button down her throat, her tongue cold and slimy against my fingers.

I held her hand. It felt like a tiny stone. "I'm so sorry." I ran to the bathroom, threw up, and screamed into the toilet bowl.

After I changed out of my wet clothes, I called Mom. "Riley's not breathing." My voice cracked at the horror of what I'd just done.

"*What?*" Mom said, panic rising in her voice. "What did she eat? There's an EpiPen in the kitchen drawer! It should stop her throat swelling. We're almost back." Mom started telling Dad to drive faster.

"No, I think she choked on something. I'm calling an ambulance." I hung up before I could hear Mom's response.

I dialed 911. If I was really doing this, I had to make it seem real. "My sister's not breathing," I said, my voice hoarse and faint. "The address is 221 Rose Street."

"I'm sending a unit right now," the operator said. "Does she have a pulse?"

"I don't know." I hung up and started to sob again, my whole body shaking. *How was this happening? Please, just let me wake from this fucked-up nightmare.*

My phone vibrated. I wiped my eyes to read the text.

Mom: What happened? Choked on what??? Is she ok???

Me: i dont know she was napping and i just found her not breathing im so sorry ambulance on the way

I hit Send, then screamed and kicked the wall.

An ambulance arrived, EMTs and a police officer rushing up the stairs to Riley's room. My stomach twisted—the police officer was Sandra Thatcher. She went to the same gym as me and Mom, high-fived us after we did burpees together. Why did I try to cover this up with a button? Officer Sandra and the EMTs would be able to tell that Riley drowned. Drowning was *not* like choking—her lungs would be full of water. *What was I thinking? What had I done? How was I this stupid?*

I put my hands to my head. Now, everyone would hate me even more for trying to cover this up. I might even go to jail for tampering with a body and lying about the fact that I'd killed my sister. And I would deserve it.

Mom and Dad sprinted into the house. I sat against the wall, burying my face in my knees. I couldn't bear to look at Mom and Dad, but I heard their screams. So primal and guttural they sounded inhuman. I covered my ears, praying for it to stop, but the sound was inescapable.

The EMTs declared Riley dead on the scene. Mom collapsed into Dad's arms, who slid slowly down the wall, and I just sat there, numb disbelief washing over me. The EMTs covered Riley's body. Surely, any moment now someone would point out that she'd drowned instead of choked. The EMTs carried her tiny body down the stairs without a word. When were they going to say something?

Sandra kneeled in front of Mom and Dad, her own eyes misty. She took their hands, then looked at me. I knew it was coming, the truth of what I'd done. I should come clean.

"I panicked. I'm so sorry," I said, my throat so tight it came out a cracking squeak. "I thought it would be better if I—" Sandra turned back to Mom. She couldn't hear me over Mom and Dad's sobs.

"Cheryl, I am so sorry." Sandra grabbed Mom's shoulder. "She choked on a button."

Dad covered his mouth. Mom let out another cry. My mouth hung open.

"Choking is one of the most common causes of child fatalities," Sandra said, her voice cracking.

"A *button*?" Mom croaked.

"Two years ago, I was called to a house where a child choked on a quarter. It's so fast and silent."

No way. This couldn't be happening.

Sandra wiped her eyes. "This was just a terrible tragedy." Sandra wrapped Mom in a hug.

Was I really getting away with it? I covered my face with my hands. I thought I'd feel relieved that I'd squirmed my way out of punishment and blame, but instantly, a new wave of despair enveloped me. I wasn't just a killer—but a slimy, manipulative one.

"Oh honey," Dad said, looking at me from across the hallway. "Come here."

I shook my head, unable to move. Unable to speak.

Mom and Dad crawled over to me. Mom put her hands on my cheeks, her mascara streaming down her face. "Vivian. This is *not* your fault."

I sobbed harder.

Mom wrapped her arms around me, pressing my face to her chest.

Dad squeezed my shoulder. "We love you so much. Don't ever think we blame you."

Mom and Dad ended up declining an autopsy. It would've cost three thousand dollars, and my parents said there was no need because they already knew how Riley died. They used the money for a funeral instead. For a tiny white coffin.

If Mom and Dad had known what I'd done, if they had known I'd lied to them in their most vulnerable moment, if they'd known it was me who'd killed Riley for some subscribers on Twitch, they wouldn't just not love me anymore. They'd hate me.

I scoot back from the desk, taking a moment to blow my nose and wipe my eyes. The viewer count keeps ticking up and up, surpassing a thousand and growing. People must be sharing this stream across platforms. Good. Let the whole world hate me.

u should kill yourself

disgusting. unfollowed

omg wtf is wrong with you

evil bitch

I don't even flinch. I've already thought the same things, and worse, about myself. But the next few chat messages—they make my breath stop.

this is the bravest thing i've ever heard someone say

made a throwaway account just to write this: 9 years ago, i committed a hit and run. never told a soul. still can't sleep through the night

my nephew drowned when my brother forgot to secure the pool gate. he still blames himself but i forgave him

I backed over my dog in the driveway. I can barely fucking live with myself. I get it

What? People get it? I never fathomed any reaction aside from pure loathing. How can someone know the truth and not think I'm the worst person alive? A choking sob escapes me. Does this mean . . . I'm not as despicable as I'd thought?

Ash: it's okay Viv. you're not the only one who's done something fucked up. this doesn't change how i feel about you at all

I smile at his words—Ash knows the truth, and he doesn't hate me. "I never thought some of you would understand—" The screen crackles and my image pixelates. I disappear for a moment, the video feed consumed by black and gray lines. "Hello?" I wipe my eyes. "Can you guys hear me?"

The camera comes back into focus and I'm in front of the screen again, smiling. Except I know I'm not smiling.

"Just kidding!" the doppelgänger says on-screen. "Gosh, I know that was a messed-up story. Dark, jeez. But that's not what happened." It plays with its hair, twirling a gray-green lock around its finger. "Let's play a game?"

No. Not now. "That's not me!" I yell at the camera, but the mic doesn't pick up my voice. The camera only shows the doppelgänger.

I type in the chat: don't listen to the stream—that's not me. I'M TELLING THE TRUTH NOW—I KILLED RILEY.

The doppelgänger's image freezes, her mouth open in a laugh, eyes wide in a creepy, excited stare. Pixels distort her face and suddenly I'm back on-screen. I wave my hand to make sure it really is me. "I shouldn't have lied!" I blurt while I have control of the camera. "I just didn't want—"

A shadow spreads across my face. The screen blurs, flickering out of focus. Then the doppelgänger's face is on-screen too, half of her face overlapping mine, so it's like I have four eyes. I move to the right and a small sliver of space forms between us, our heads side by side. I glance to my left to make sure she's not really there, and no, she's not. She's inside the video itself.

WTF??

is twitch glitching?

Viv r there 2 of u

is this a mirror filter? wats it called

is this whole thing a joke

Ash: i don't like this, Viv, get out of the house

"I didn't want everyone to hate me," I say. "I'm so sorry."

"It wasn't my fault," the doppelgänger says, speaking at the same time as me. "She choked."

"I LIED!" I scream. "I put the button down her throat, like a monster!"

"No, she really just choked—" The doppelgänger tries to speak again, but her voice is quieter than mine.

The screen goes black. I jiggle the mouse, but the computer is off. I scoot back from the desk, trying to slow my breathing. I need to read the chat messages again. I press the desktop's power button, rebooting the computer.

The screen turns on to gray static, the speakers emitting white noise. Oh, come on. The center of my monitor wavers, like it's turning to liquid. *What the hell?* I blink a few times to make sure my vision's not just blurry. The screen is def undulating, like it's some sort of portal. A pale hand reaches through. My heart leaps. An arm sticks out through the screen, fingers gripping the edge of the desk.

Oh fuck. My body tells me to run, but I can't move.

The hand pulls forward and a head comes through the screen—*my* head, the face grinning wickedly. There's a cracking sound, and the doppelgänger pulls through the monitor, shoulders sagging unevenly, neck straining to fit. The rest of her body crawls through the screen and she tumbles to the floor, her body twisted. *Shit, shit, shit.* I find my legs and back up against the wall.

The doppelgänger slowly stands, her bones cracking into place in quick rapid succession, dislocated shoulders snapping back into their joint sockets. An urge to vomit rolls through my stomach. My phone vibrates on the desk; Ash is calling me. But I can't reach it. The doppelgänger takes a shaky, uneven step toward me.

I scream for Mom and Dad. They're just down the hall in their room.

"They can't hear you." The doppelgänger steps closer, a shit-eating grin on her face.

"Mom! Dad!" I shout as loud as I can, but they're not coming.

"No one can hear you in here."

Goddamn it. "Leave me alone! You win! I told everyone my darkest secret—everyone hates me now!" But I know that's not true. I glance beside me, looking for a weapon but there's just clothes and *Pokémon* plushies. Why couldn't I have collected something useful like swords? I don't even have that stupid dagger anymore.

"Today," the doppelgänger says in my voice, "you're going to kill yourself."

I shake my head.

"Because you can't stand the guilt anymore." The doppelgänger's eyes flicker with excitement. "Mommy and Daddy are going to find you hanged in your room." She lurches for me.

I sidestep to avoid her, and she steps into the rays of sunlight beaming through the window. Something looks different about her—she's gaunt. Her face is still mine, but the cheekbones are extra bony, and spots on her neck are mottled, like she's starting to rot.

She lunges again and I jump out of the way. But why am I fighting back? Shouldn't I let her kill me so everyone else can be safe?

She makes another grab for me and this time I'm too slow. Her fingers wrap around my throat. I close my eyes, expecting her to squeeze my head off with that death grip of hers, but her grasp on me isn't nearly as strong as it was the night before.

"Precious Mommy and Daddy won't be able to stand the memory of you when they know the truth."

She's right. Ash and a few Twitch strangers might be sympathetic, but Mom and Dad will never forgive me for killing their baby.

The doppelgänger takes a deep inhale, her eyes fluttering, like I'm a delicious meal. Her grip tightens and I start to give in. *Then after I'm dead, Mom and Dad will see my confession and they can start to move on with their lives.*

The doppelgänger's other hand reaches for my neck, but this one is completely rotten, pieces of pale skin dangling from dark, bleeding flesh. Her greenish-gray hair is thinning, revealing a scaly scalp. She's so ugly I look away from her. My eyes focus on Riley's picture on my desk, at her smile with those two little teeth. I feel that swell of guilt again. The doppelgänger's hair thickens. Her grip doubles in strength. My fingers automatically try to pry her off my neck so I can breathe. Even though I know I should die, my body wants to live. Why does my body have to be so annoyingly persistent? *Just let me die, dammit.* The doppelgänger's grip overpowers my resistance, clamping off my airway. Finally. White spots flash in my eyes.

But how is she getting stronger? I wonder in a lack-of-oxygen haze. I know my monsters—something must be feeding her, fueling her like a mana source.

The room spins.

I fall to my knees, the doppelgänger still strangling me, my vision fading to black.

I see Mom and Dad in the hallway when Riley was pronounced dead, the way Mom shook her head and said, "No, she's not. She can't be." Her body began to sway, her knees trembling. She collapsed onto Dad. Mom cried all through the night. "I should've looked for that button," she wailed. "I should've found it."

And what did I do? Nothing. I let Mom blame herself. And she's been blaming herself ever since. How will she and Dad take it when they come home tonight and find my dead body in my room? I didn't think about that before. All I wanted was for it to be over.

But of course, they're going to blame themselves for that too.

Can I really do that to them again? Can I really leave them childless?

That night Riley died, after her body was taken and the first responders left, Dad pulled me and Mom onto the couch, embracing us in a hug. "Neither of you are at fault here," he said. Those were the words I clung to, the ones I let fester and fuel my guilt. I'd forgotten the words he said next:

"We love you so much, Vivian. We don't know what we'd do without you."

How can I abandon them now? How can I leave them with two dead kids?

My lungs burn and scream for air, but it's too late. I'm dying. I'm really dying.

I'm so sorry, Mom, Dad, and Riley. If I could go back and save you, I would, a thousand times over.

I loved you, Riley.

I should've taken better care of you.

I miss you so much.

I miss your little laugh and your pet worms and your gluten-free bread that really wasn't so bad.

For the first time in all these terrible months since she died, instead of that sickening guilt, I'm overcome by a new sensation: grief. Overwhelming waves of sadness for the little sister I lost.

I never wanted you to die.

I didn't mean for it to happen.

I fucked up.

And that's not the same as killing someone, is it? No. Riley's death was just a horrible accident.

Air seeps into my lungs, a sweet rush of brilliant light to my chest. My eyes flutter open. What the hell is happening? My vision focuses. I'm lying on the floor of my room. The doppelgänger is still holding my neck, but her grasp is weak. I almost scream looking at her, but my throat is too raw.

My face is sagging off the demon's skull, my cheeks drooping, eyebrows sliding down sideways, eyelids hanging where the nose should be. The skin begins to slough away, dripping to the floor like melting flesh-colored ice cream, revealing the mottled brown and blackened flesh beneath. And then it clicks—this is what it's been feeding on: my guilt for Riley. Of course. My goddamn self-loathing, pity party guilt.

"I didn't mean to kill Riley," I croak. "It was an accident." I climb to my knees, prying at the demon's fingers on my neck. I don't know if I can ever really forgive myself, but if I could undo Riley's death, I would, and the fact I regret it so badly, that has to stand for something, right? Don't people live with terrible regrets all the time? I think of all the letters Ash's dad sends to him, how Ash still writes back even though his dad literally ran people over. If Ash can forgive his dad, can my parents forgive me? I think of the Twitch chat, of all those people who've made horrible mistakes, and still they go on with their lives. Maybe I can too. The doppelgänger's fingers snap backward, and it shrieks, letting go of my neck.

I inhale another full breath of air and stand. The doppelgänger straightens its hand, broken fingers slowly snapping back into place. It stands, too, hunched over, the ridges of its spine visible through its thin, mottled flesh. It lunges for me, claws swiping at my neck, but it's slower and instead of letting it hit me, I dodge to the side because the truth is: I don't want to die. I don't want to leave Mom and Dad devastated and alone, and even beyond that, there's still so much I want to do with my life. I want to visit cat cafés with my parents in Japan and write my own video game and see Bri become a lawyer and kiss Ash again and again. Just because Riley doesn't get to do any of the things she might have wanted, does it really mean I have to give up my life too?

The last patches of my hair fall from the demon's scalp, sizzling and disappearing into the floor. "*You think you deserve to live even though you killed your sister?*" it says in its awful deep voice, black tongue flickering between its teeth.

"Kind of, yeah."

It lurches at me with its clawed hand, but I smack it out of the way. The demon hisses.

"I killed my baby sister," it says in a small, girly voice. "My parents went to Chicago for a play, and I promised I wouldn't stream any video games, but I did, and I forgot about my sister and left the bathtub full and she drowned while I was playing *Morgue Mayhem*—"

My stomach drops. It's quoting what I typed in the game.

"When I realized she was dead, I shoved a button down her throat to make it look like it wasn't my fault."

I want to cover my ears, but I don't. I didn't mean for Riley to die. I've never allowed myself to even consider this before, but the truth is—it was an accident. What I did next was reprehensible, but I was panicked and terrified, and didn't want my parents to hate me.

"Yeah, that's right," I deadpan. "She died and I covered it up." I inhale a shaky breath. "I fucked up. Really bad." I wipe my eyes.

The demon flinches, its claws retracting into its hands. It takes a step backward toward the computer. It's not retreating, right? I can't let it get away. It could recharge and come after me again. I have to end this. I don't have any weapons, but I have my hands. If this were an RPG, I'd be -2 in unarmed combat, but my enemy's weakened.

I lunge forward before the demon can get to the desk. My

hands wrap around its stringy, decaying neck. I clamp down, trying to strangle it, but I don't think this thing even breathes. A claw slices my shoulder. My skin ignites in pain, but I don't let go. The demon tries to bite me, its beady orange eyes widening.

Eyes. The universal weak spot.

I press my thumbs into its pupils. My thumbs give way, digging into cold, gelatinous tissue. *Ew, ew, ew.*

The demon thrashes, its claws slashing my arms. My shirt tears, cuts erupting across my skin. I ignore the pain and dig my thumbs in deeper, aiming for its brain or whatever's behind those eyes. The demon screeches, and it begins to shorten, its legs dissolving into a black, sludgy pile on the ground.

I bend down to its height, still pressing my fingers into the demon's eyes, crushing its head between my hands. The demon lets out a long, shrill wail, its black tongue lashing slowly between its teeth. Then the rest of its body joins the puddle on the floor, melting into a tar-like substance.

Now what? Do I . . . mop it up? Or . . . ? The black sludge starts wriggling toward the desk. I stomp on it. *Die! Die! Die!*

My bedroom door bangs open. Ash rushes to me. "Viv—are you okay? What happened?"

"It tried to kill me. I think it's dying."

He puts his arm around me, and together we watch as the black sludge fizzles into the floor.

I stand at the edge of the living room, wearing a big sweatshirt, the choke marks on my neck concealed with makeup. Mom and Dad are on the couch, sharing a bag of chips and watching *The Office*. They look so peaceful, like their lives haven't been in utter chaos these last few weeks. I don't want to disturb this moment, but I have to. If I'm going to live with myself, if I'm going to be sure the demon is really gone, and simply because I don't want to keep it from them anymore: I'm going to tell the truth about Riley.

"Mom, Dad—"

Their heads whip toward me. Dad turns the TV down, giving me a soft smile.

"We thought you were sleeping," Mom says. "We have good news."

"What?"

"Bri is okay; she's expected to make a full recovery."

I nod. Bri already texted me that she was awake and watched my stream. She said she's proud of me for telling the truth, and she most definitely doesn't hate me. We're still best friends, now and forever.

"She told the police that it wasn't you," Mom continues, "and the cops found surveillance footage that shows you by the swing set at the time Bri was stabbed. The actual culprit's face isn't visible in the security footage by the gazebo, but the police agree that the witnesses were mistaken. They aren't pursuing charges against you." Mom wipes her eyes.

Dad stands up, hugging me. "I'm sorry I didn't believe you. It's just, with all that's been going on—"

"It's okay. I have something I need to tell you too."

Dad squeezes my shoulders. "Are you sick? Your voice sounds awful."

"Yeah." I'm thankful my hoarseness passes for a cold and not just-got-strangled-to-the-brink-of-death-by-a-demon. "Getting the flu or something." I sit on the sofa chair across from them and wait for Dad to return to his spot on the couch. I thought about just showing them the Twitch recording so I wouldn't have to say it all over again, but that didn't feel right, so I deleted it.

They deserve to hear the words from me in person.

"So, what I wanted to say is that—" I pause, forcing myself to look Mom in the eyes. "I lied about Riley's death."

Mom's body tenses, her face going pale. Dad's jaw clenches.

"That weekend you left, you told me not to go on Twitch." The words are like glue sealing my throat shut. "But I did anyway. Riley got sorbet all over herself and I was going to give her a bath. I filled the tub, but then I forgot about it and left her alone." My voice quivers. "Riley drowned while I was on Twitch."

Mom covers her mouth, tears rolling down her cheeks, leaking between her fingers. Dad bends forward, covering his face.

Here it comes, the hatred.

Dad gets up without looking at me and walks through the kitchen into the garage. Oh no. What is he doing? Gathering boxes to make me move out? Or what if he's calling the cops on me?

Mom bends over, crying into her hands. "Oh my god," she says. "Oh my god."

"Mom—"

She shakes her head, still sobbing.

"It wasn't my button," Mom mutters. "It wasn't me."

I wrap my arms around myself. My parents will probably never speak to me again.

A minute later, Dad returns, wiping his eyes with the backs of his hands. "Come here."

I step forward, uncertain. What is he going to do? Throw me out of the house?

Dad wraps me in a hug. Mom stands, hugging me too. And for a long moment, they just hold me.

"Thank you for telling us," Mom says, her voice strained.

"Do you hate me?"

My parents step back to look at me.

"Honey," Mom's voice tightens, "of course we don't hate you."

"But I got Riley killed, and I made up that story about her choking." I look down. "On *your* button."

Mom and Dad are quiet for a moment, then Mom speaks. "I'm angry." She pauses to blow her nose. "And hurt."

My stomach clenches.

"But I remember what it was like to be your age, and if I'd made the same mistake, I might've lied about it too."

Mom turns to Dad, who nods in agreement.

"It doesn't change the facts. Riley's still . . ." Dad swallows. "Gone. But we have you. And telling the truth about a lie like that? That takes real maturity and bravery."

I stare at them, my mouth open. I never expected this. I could almost laugh with relief. Mom gives me a soft smile. She must feel so much better now, knowing it was all my fault and never hers.

Mom puts her arm around me, pulling me close. "You don't ever have to lie to us, okay?"

"People make mistakes," Dad says. "We know you didn't mean to hurt Riley, and when we said we didn't blame you, we still mean it now."

The tightness in my chest loosens. I rest my head on his shoulder.

Dad squeezes me. "We love you, Vivian."

Ash seals a strip of tape on the box containing my shoes, then places it on top of the others marked Viv's clothes, Viv's stuffed animals, Viv's misc. things.

Bri pinches the sleeves of a green turtleneck sweater, holding it up like it's filth. "Goodwill. Absolutely Goodwill."

"I trust you." I nod at her.

Bri tosses it into the donation basket.

"Thanks for helping, guys," I say. "You really didn't have to give up your Saturday."

"Like I wouldn't take this opportunity to clean out your closet." Bri pulls another shirt off its hanger. Pink scars spread up her arms. The nerves on her right hand took a lot of damage, so she struggles with fine motor skills like typing. The doctors said that with physical therapy, there's hope she'll regain full function, but no guarantee. I almost want to blame myself for that too, but I'm done feeling guilty for things outside my control. The doppelgänger did that to Bri, not me.

"What about this?" Ash plucks the webcam off my monitor.

"Goodwill."

"*Really?*" Bri gasps.

"What? It's not like I'm giving up gaming. Just don't want to keep up with all the performances."

"Alright." Ash smiles, placing the webcam in the Goodwill box.

I pick the Christmas picture of me and Riley off the desk, wrapping it in newspaper. Everyone knows that I killed Riley now, but they don't think of it that way. They still think of it as a sad, horrible accident. I was the only one who thought of myself as a murderer.

"Packing going well in here?" Mom asks, popping her head into my room.

"Making good progress." I smile, gesturing at all the piles of stuff.

"Great. An hour until a pizza break." She follows the movers down the stairs.

I squat to pick up the heaviest box full of makeup and hair and skin products, and I hand it to Ash.

He takes it from me and groans. "What the hell is in this?"

"Just a few things that keep me beautiful." I smirk, picking up a box of clothes. Bri grabs one as well, then the three of us walk downstairs, passing Dad, who's helping the movers carry the couch out the door to the U-Haul.

I place my box on the front lawn.

"You think you'll like Des Moines?" Ash asks, dropping his box with a heavy thud next to mine.

I shrug. "They have a Cheesecake Factory."

"I'm just going to miss you so much," Bri whines.

"I'm going to miss you too." An HVAC company recruited Dad to be their new foreman, and we all need a fresh start. Bri's attacker was never caught, obviously, and several of our classmates believe I really was the stabber. I doubt those rumors have reached as far as every corner in Des Moines, but even if they have, then that means no one will fuck with me. There's a bright side to everything.

"It's only an hour away," Ash says. "We're used to driving long distances by now."

I crack a smile. "Exactly. We'll swap weekends."

I wrap my arms around Ash's neck, pressing my lips against his, his mouth minty and fresh from all the gum he chews to distract from the nicotine withdrawal. He brushes my hair back, tucking the loose locks behind my ear. I'm going to miss him, and I'm going to miss hanging out with Bri every day, but I know the three of us will text constantly and play new indie co-op games and *Magic*, and more than I'm sad about this move, I'm ready.

Ready to begin my new life, unburdened.

EPILOGUE

"Players need to be able to choose their ghost's starting power," Dennis says. "Not have the game pick it for them."

"The ghost's power should be determined by the player's cause of death," I say. "That's the RPG aspect of the first act."

Half the game design team nods, but a few glance toward Dennis, clearly taking his side.

My idea is better, but I remind myself that this is a *team* project. "Let's just put a pin in that."

"How are we on map design?" Dennis asks.

"We have seven neighborhoods sketched out, each one with a different theme," Lucy says. She continues, talking about the different spawn points and unique locations. I keep listening while scrolling through Instagram on my phone.

I open Bri's story: She's wearing a form-fitting light blue dress, posing on the sidewalk in Times Square, a Birthday Girl sash wrapped around her shoulders. Her scars have healed well, the one on her right shoulder is entirely concealed with a new butterfly tattoo. She just turned nineteen and is over the moon to be starting at Columbia next month. I type: can't wait to visit!!!! and hit Send, then I scroll through my feed.

Ash posted a pic of himself smiling in front of a white, regal museum in Acapulco, his sandy-blond hair cut short. Right after graduation, he started applying for crewman jobs on freight ships in every state along the coast and got hired by some place in Florida. Sounds absolutely miserable to me, but he's been doing it for a couple months, and on our FaceTimes he's said he gets to sightsee after work, makes more money than if he'd gotten a bachelor's degree, and enjoys seeing the world beyond Iowa. But he'll be back for his week off soon. We already have our tickets to the state fair.

"Viv? Hellooo?" Lucy says, waving at me. "What do you think of the character designs?"

My attention snaps back to the game design group. Dennis clicks through the sample photos on his laptop.

"Not bad," I say. We have a handful of generic 2D characters with a range of skin colors and body types . . . but they also look like they're from a 2008 PS2 game. "Maybe a little goofy in the eyes." The eyes are way too big. "Let's fix that?"

"Fine, but only if players get to choose their starting power." Dennis smirks.

"Yeah, but don't blame me when the reviewers hate that."

I met Lucy and Dennis in my Des Moines high school's video game club, and now that we've just graduated, we spend the hours we're not on the clock at the local coffee shop designing our own horror RPG. I don't know if we'll ever get the funds to actually get this thing off the ground, but a girl can hope. Maybe the Kickstarter will take off—it just takes the right person to share it.

"Do we have any new working titles?" Dennis asks. "We're not calling it *Kingdom of Ghosts: The Reckoning* anymore, right?"

"I liked that one." Lucy pouts. "But we can look at new indie horrors for inspiration if we want a flashier name." She changes the page on Dennis's laptop from the character designs to Twitch. I haven't streamed since I gave it up last year, but I check out which new indie games are making the streamer rounds regularly. It's the best way to see what's trending and plan how to position our game in the market. I might get back into streaming someday, but for now, the coffee shop pays my bills, and it's nice to just game for 100 percent fun and 0 percent business.

Lucy slowly scrolls through the horror games, reading off titles. "*Band of Bones. The Mystery of Apartment B. Locked In. Eaten Alive.*"

"*Wait*," I say, standing so fast my chair knocks back. "Go back."

"*The Mystery of Apartment*—"

"No. *Locked In.* What's the full name?"

She scrolls back to it. LOCKED IN: An Escape Room Horror Game.

My tongue turns dry, pulse throbbing in my neck.

"Open the stream," I say.

Dennis scoffs. "Really? It looks like cheap 2010 garbage."

"Play it!"

Lucy loads the stream.

A purple-haired teen girl sits in a gaming chair, giggling on camera. She can't be older than sixteen. Her avatar walks down a dark abandoned hallway and unlocks a door marred with scratches. She steps inside. My heart knocks in my chest.

A grandfather clock ticks in the corner. A cloaked figure sits on the stained couch.

"Oooh, creepy grandpa." The streamer girl giggles.

"Really, why are we watching this?" Dennis gestures in annoyance. "Our game isn't anything like this."

The girl walks her avatar closer to the couch. Beady orange eyes stare back at her from beneath the hood. My heart leaps, pulse drumming in my ears.

No way. I killed that thing. It's dead. Gone. I crushed its head in my hands, and it gurgled into black sludge on the floor and disappeared. The image replays in my dreams every night. My stomach knots. Or did I just send it back to the place it came from?

The NPC stands, taking staggering, jerky steps closer to the girl's avatar. Words type across the screen.

Tell me a secret.

THE END

ACKNOWLEDGMENTS

Thank you to everyone who helped bring this book to life:

My wonderful agent, Amanda Orozco, who's believed in this story since my rambling "it's like *The Ring* but with a video game" pitch.

My editor, Tamara Grasty, for championing this novel and pushing me to dig even deeper into its layers of guilt and horror.

My copyeditor, Heather Taylor, for fixing my egregious usage of "lay" instead of "lie."

The Page Street team, for their brilliant minds and dedication to their authors: Cas Jones, Rosie Stewart, Meg Palmer, Hayley Gundlach, Caitlyn Boyd, Emma Hardy, and Jane Horovitz. My writing group, The UberGroup—especially Katherine Jennings for reading multiple drafts, revisions, and answering many panicked midnight messages.

Meredith Tate, Sushannah Smith, and AE Kade for reading the very first draft.

Michael Marquez, who's helped form each of my book ideas through a series of text messages.

I'd also like to thank my wonderful colleagues and instructors from the Nonfiction Writing Program at the University of Iowa. To Kerry Howley, for always being the voice in my head asking, "What is this really about?" To Inara Verzemnieks, John

D'Agata, and Brooks Landon for their unwavering belief in my abilities. To my cohort, who graciously welcomed every dark, twisty thing I brought to workshop. To Gabriela Tully Claymore, Carey Dunne, Gyasi Hall, Jessie Kraemer, Jenny Fran Davis, and Sanjna Singh for their emotional support and insistence that I celebrate my successes. To Jonathan Gleason for many late-night book talks and for always being a trusted reader.

Thank you to Versa Fitness for being the best day job an author could ask for, and to every member who's asked me how the book is coming along. Thank you to all my early readers, loved ones, friends, and coworkers who've supported and believed in me: Jordon Walter, Jean Geisberg, Jordin Butcher, Randie Butcher, Megan Lind Persinger, Brittany DeBeeld, Laura Creedle, Nick Burrell, Josh Lambrecht, and more!

ABOUT THE AUTHOR

Tatiana Schlote-Bonne holds an MFA from the Nonfiction Writing Program at the University of Iowa. When she's not writing, she's either gaming, lifting heavy weights, or teaching people how to lift heavy weights. *Such Lovely Skin* is her debut novel.